'Hang the robbers!'

There was no ceremony; t̲l̲............g̲h̲t̲.
The crowd pushed forward. ......ɑɪɪ screamed that she was being crushed but none heeded her. Others stretched up to their full height so that they might be afforded a clearer view.

It was all over in the winking of an eye. The moonman's weight was instrumental in breaking his neck instantly. There was a delay as his executioners struggled to free his corpse, dragged it to one side. The second victim was already being pulled up the steps to the gallows.

This one was lighter. His frailty prolonged his agony, a choking and kicking figure who finally drowned in his own vomit.

The third man's neck was skinned and stretched, until his death throes resembled those of an ostrich. The fourth had an uncanny resistance to death; the constables crowded round his twitching body, and the dull thuds which reached the strained ears of the watchers indicated that he had been dispatched by clubbing.

The crowd whistled and jeered; a pleasure that should have been prolonged and savoured had, instead, been hastily and clumsily brought to a conclusion.

They watched the bodies being loaded on to the charnel cart, did not even notice the swarming flies.

'Bring out the witch. *Burn the witch!'*

also by Gavin Newman

The Hangman

An Unholy Way to Die

Gavin Newman

Bulldog Books
A Division of Black Hill Books

Bulldog Books
A Division of Black Hill Books
PO Box 23, Knighton, Powys LD7 1WS

A Bulldog paperback original 1999
Copyright © Gavin Newman 1999

ISBN 0 9532701 3 0

Typesetting by Hal C. F. Astell, Halifax

Cover illustration by Andrew Compton

For Robert Adey, a good friend and
a master of the Locked Room mystery

This is more strange than such a murder is;
There, the murderers,
Steep'd in the colours of their trade,
Their daggers unmannerly breech'd with gore.

— William Shakespeare

CHAPTER ONE

The old man shuffled down the street, a bowed ragbag figure in the half-light of a summer dawn, his skeletal legs scarcely able to support the weight of his emaciated body. Barefooted, his blackened and broken toenails scuffed the dirt, and his long arms dangling by his side gave an appearance of physical deformity.

'Hurry, Ned.' The gruff voice behind him spoke with urgency. 'You have to be in the stocks by dawn else the churchwarden will want to know the reason, and we're late already.'

Ned stumbled, almost lost his balance, half turned to glance behind him, grunted an unintelligible reply through cracked and blistered lips. He had no fear of the constable for, in his own rough way, Bill Symes was kindly enough, a man whose job depended upon not incurring the wrath of the churchwarden. The law called for a purge on vagrants and begging carried a punishment of daylight hours spent in the agony and ignominy of the stocks. The constable had no choice but to enforce that law.

But Ned feared the officer's dog, a huge rough beast of wolfhound strain, a creature that growled from deep in its slavering jaws and lusted for beggars with the same appetite it showed for bones in the gutters. Its eyes peered from behind a shaggy curtain of straggling hair, glared with a ferocity that was only kept in check by its master's staff. Hackles raised because it scented the rancid body odours which it associated with starving itinerants, it kept pace with its owner whilst willing his command to 'gerr'um!' It had not forgotten last week when it had been ordered to chase a band of Romanies from the town. Their nut-brown flesh had a flavour similar to that of beggars. Akin to farm livestock.

Somehow Ned kept ahead of man and dog, a stagger that maintained a momentum. He clawed at an itching beneath his wisping grey beard – the lice were active this morning.

'Let's hope the churchwarden is still abed.' Symes glanced up and down the deserted street, adjusted his high-crowned hat, a habit of his when he was nervous. His bulky frame was imposing in its uniform, an embroidered scarlet coat to match his canions, and jet-black nether socks. If the townspeople resented him, they certainly respected him and that was all that mattered.

Down Chapel Street and into High Street. The daylight was coming fast now; there was already a roseate streak in the grey eastern sky. Symes muttered beneath his breath. He was beginning to blow with his thick lips.

Then he gave a faintly audible sigh of relief as the stark silhouette of the Market Cross loomed up ahead like some squat house on stilts. Beneath were wooden benches in readiness for the market; traders would be arriving within the hour to set out their stalls — clothing and food, mostly. Benjamin, the wandering pedlar, was always to be seen on Fridays with an array of pomanders, mirrors, gloves, cards and trinkets, anything which might take the fancy of an impromptu buyer and persuade them to part with hard-earned wages in a moment of rashness.

Benjamin was cheeky; oft times the constable had feinted a cuff at the other's ear. But there was no law against peddling. Just begging.

'Get yer hands through.' Symes lifted the top board of the stocks, pushed the beggar down into a kneeling position. 'Head forward. That's it!'

Ned was so scrawny that there was always the possibility that he might be able to drag his talon-like hands back through the apertures, but there was no way he could free his head. The old man was shaking as if he had the ague. The constable fought off a feeling of pity; Ned knew full well the consequences of begging, had been in the stocks before. Begging wasn't necessary. Shelters had been built for the homeless under the Poor Laws, and the Church provided them with a bowl of soup or gruel each evening. God save the Queen, the bishop and the Lord Lieutenant, too. A few years ago the likes of Ned would have been left to starve or else make a nuisance of themselves asking for sustenance on the streets. Nowadays begging was just greed.

'You'll do.' Symes stood back and surveyed his prisoner. The other was resting his chin on the hole; by nightfall his neck would be as stiff as a corpse's, his features unrecognisable beneath a morass of broken rotten eggs and squelchy fruit. Some of the produce traders made an extra few pence by selling their overripe wares to revellers from the ale houses. The stocks were an added attraction to the market, like skittles at the sideshows when the fair came to town.

Ned belched, a hollow sound that came in a rush from an empty stomach. When the hour came for his release all the Church handouts would long have been consumed, the bowls licked clean in readiness for the morrow. He would not dare to beg again.

'Quiet!' Symes aimed a kick at his growling companion but the dog was experienced in dodging the heavy boot. Its head turned, its ears cocked up. It had sensed, rather than heard, somebody approaching. Maybe it was the first of the traders arriving.

The figure that came into view was no seller of wares; the very piety of his posture was evidence of that. Hands clasped in front of him, head bowed so that his tonsured crown was clearly visible. His step was slow and measured, the wide-sleeved black woollen habit swung with his movements, the sandalled feet made scarcely a footfall on the road.

'Brother Edmund, what brings you here at this hour?' Symes spoke authoritatively yet with a tone of respect. Only too well he recognised the homeless monk who had arrived in town early in the spring and stayed.

There were whispered rumours about the stranger, that he had been expelled from a monastery up north for acts of indiscretion with his brothers; that his faith had wavered and he had taken to the roads to find it again. Supposition was rife but one let malicious alehouse gossip go unheeded. All the same, the monk was not to be fully trusted until he had proved himself, and sleeping with the poor in their crude shelter was no way to endear oneself to the honest townspeople.

Edmund lifted his head, revealing rotund features that in no way bore the ravages of near starvation. The flesh was pink and smooth, the lips forced a smile. 'This is no way to treat the starving, constable, nor the old and infirm.'

'Ned is old, but he is neither ill nor starving. He was begging for food in addition to that which the Church in its generosity provides. Is not greed a sin, brother?'

The dog growled hesitantly as if for some reason it was afraid of the newcomer. Its scraggy tail curled between its hindquarters, remained there. It backed off a yard, looked as though it might flee.

'Greed is eating more than you need.'

The constable was uncertain of himself. His job was to uphold the law, not to enter into philosophical discussions.

'Depending upon your needs. Or amassing riches beyond the necessities of life.'

'That is dangerous talk, monk.' Symes's features flushed.

11

'Only if the garment fits.' Edmund smiled disarmingly. 'I merely state what I have learned in a life devoted to God. I am but His humble servant, I ask no more than to do His bidding and to be granted shelter and enough food.'

'You do not seem to have gone short of food,' the constable's lips curled, 'judging by the flesh under your chin and the way your belly protrudes!' Rising anger transcended discretion and respect. This fellow was no more than a vagrant, his holy orders probably a façade. He might be a coney-catcher in the guise of a monk.

'I have learned to live off the fruits of the wayside and woodlands.' Edmund was unmoved, smiling again. 'And in return for charity I spread the word of God. One who lives humbly has a better understanding of life. I beg you to release that man, constable.'

'I cannot, I dare not. Go speak with Martyn Wylde, the churchwarden, see if your pleadings will move him to compassion. The law is the law, my duty is to enforce it. I am answerable directly to the churchwarden.'

Edmund shook his head sadly. He turned, met the gaze of the man in the stocks, the silent plea for mercy. The hooked nose, encrusted with blackheads like barnacles on the bows of a ship, snorted as the sufferer gasped for breath. Ned might well not live to see his freedom at the end of the day.

'It is a barbaric punishment, as was Our Lord's upon the Cross. Crowd hysteria, baying for the death of the innocent, condoned by those who purport to have the good of the people at heart.'

'Go talk to Wylde, but watch your tongue, else you might be in the stocks tomorrow!' Symes turned away. The dog circled to avoid the monk, slunk to heel. 'And one more thing, don't you go interfering with Ned. Feeding a prisoner in the stocks is forbidden by law, the churchwarden will tell you that. Three days' imprisonment if you do.'

'I shall keep an eye on him, nothing more,' the other promised. 'If his health deteriorates then I shall request that a physician is summoned.'

'Have you the money to pay a physician?'

'No, but he will be rewarded when his time comes.'

'Pah, you are wasting my time talking nonsense. Only the churchwarden can authorise treatment of a prisoner and Wylde won't do that for a vagrant. I warn you, keep away from him. Now, I have work to do. The town will be crowded and there will be drunks in every ale house.'

'Drinking too much is greed,' the monk's tone was almost patronising, 'which is a sin, so I must not delay you from your work, constable.'

Symes strode away, the dog cringing close to his heels. For some inexplicable canine reason it was terrified of the holy man, but that was no concern of the constable's.

Markets were becoming busier in Stratford. People flocked from far afield, villages such as Tiddington, Alveston, Ludding, Welford and others. The number of stalls was increasing; on fine days they lined the street beyond the Market Cross. There was talk of another covered area being built, but that would depend upon Lord Armdale; such matters were left to the jurisdiction of the lord of the manor.

Strangers from London were to be seen about the town, for performances of the bard's plays in the capital had attracted unprecedented attention and now Stratford was becoming known nationally. Even those who had no interest in the stage accepted that it was good for trade.

By mid-morning the streets were filled with jostling crowds; peasant women in their rough garb, ladies with richly embroidered doublets and lace-edged ruffles worn over exaggeratedly full skirts. Rings, necklaces and earrings proclaimed the wealth of the wearers. Peasant men in slops, yeomen and tenant farmers wearing trunk hoses with canions, peasecod-bellied doublets and piccadills – an array of finery and contrasting colours when simpler garb would have been more comfortable in the heat of the day. Market days were fast becoming more than just times for trading and bartering of wares: they were opportunities to demonstrate one's status where previously it had gone unnoticed.

The ale houses were already full, the overspill seated on benches outside drinking a variety of locally brewed ales and ciders. Edmund mingled with the crowds thronging the Market Cross, attracted glances of mild curiosity. A wandering monk was not unknown in the town but there was always a lurking suspicion shrouding his presence. A man of God commanded respect; you left him well alone.

Nicholas, the coney-catcher, watched with furtive eyes as he lounged against a weathered oaken support. He was smartly dressed, at a distance his tassets giving the appearance of a suit of armour. Slight of build, his wits were as quick as his slender hands when the opportunity arose. Oft times women carried money in their shopping baskets, and whilst their attention was diverted by tempting wares or gossip it was an easy matter to extract it without their knowledge.

He kept a wary eye out for the constable. Only last month a thief had been hanged, a common rogue with neither guile nor sleight of hand. The fellow had paid dearly for his foolishness in being caught, not for his theft. It was a motto that was ever present in Nicholas's mind.

A crowd had gathered in front of the stocks, a medley of youths who were spared one day a month from their labours in the fields and were bent on mischievous pleasure. Already they had tipped up Barnaby's vegetable cart, mocked the trader for his wrath. His shouts for the constable had gone unheard in the babble of market noise. In all probability Symes was confining his duties to upholding the law in the ale houses; he would not be seen until later.

The stocks were legitimate pleasure. One was actively encouraged to participate in bombarding the unfortunate prisoner with objects of a noxious but unharmful nature. Eggs and vegetables which had remained unsold from the previous week were offered at a penny for as many as you could carry. The youths helped themselves liberally; the crowd parted in anticipation of a stinking bombardment of the unfortunate human target.

Ned's eyes were closed. He had slumped against the boards, hung there by his wasted hands. His chin supported his scabby head. Perhaps, even at the height of his discomfort, he slept in the heat of the day.

A ragged yokel with protruding teeth and a shock of unkempt red hair weighed a muck-encrusted goose egg in his grimy hand, tossed it and caught it for effect. He looked round to ensure that he had the attention of his colleagues.

'Back a pace, Pouk!' A tall youth with a fluff of growth on his chin guffawed. 'It's no feat from that distance.'

'Back three then!' The one called Pouk took three deliberate paces backwards. At the autumn fair he had felled three swedes out of four from twice this distance. 'Right?'

'What're you waitin' for, Pouk?' Guffaws from the audience. 'Tryin' to 'atch that egg in yer 'and? It's addled, it won't 'atch!'

The back of Pouk's neck reddened, his arm went back, poised. Then it shot forward with every ounce of strength his lean body could muster.

Ned's head jerked up from its recumbent posture, the features instantly unrecognisable beneath a morass of slimy dark yellow, a sluggish river of addled yolk oozing from the crown, hanging like phlegm from the hooked nose. His lips parted, gave forth a sound that might have been a wheeze or a groan, spat feebly at the sticky substance in an attempt to clear it. Coughing, choking.

Then a stench of concentrated putrefaction had the onlookers stepping back.

'Bullseye, Pouk!'

'Let me go next.' The tall youth pushed his way forward, held up another egg. 'Watch!'

A figure detached itself from the crowd, moved with a dignified urgency to stand between the beggar and the throwers. The wide sleeve fell back as a soft pink hand was upraised. Edmund's expression was one of concern and pity rather than anger.

'I beg you to cease.' His tone was almost musical, as if he was chanting the catechism. 'In the name of God, stop this senseless assault on a harmless old man. Ned has done you no wrong.'

'Out of the way, monk!' The tall youth drew his arm up above his head. 'He's a beggar and all beggars must go in the stocks. It is the law.'

'I shall not move.' The homeless monk smiled. 'If it is the law that beggars are put in the stocks then he must remain there until he is freed at nightfall. But I shall see that he is not harmed throughout his period of captivity.'

The youth glanced behind him at his companions. The one named Pouk grinned, winked. 'We can't help it if the monk got in the way, can we, Tom?'

The egg struck Edmund with full force, exploded its rotten contents all over his face. He reeled but regained his balance, wiped his face with his sleeve. And when he spoke again there was not so much as a tremor in his voice. 'Throw at me, then. Rather that than at a sick old man.'

Shouts and whistles came from the gathering and next second a fusillade of eggs and rotted cabbages rained on the one who attempted to deprive them of their sport. Cabbages *thwacked* against the stout body, left decomposing leaves adhering to the rough wool of the habit as they bounced off. Eggs burst like *grenados* on his head and face.

'Shame on you!' A woman's voice screeched from amidst the onlookers. 'Can you not see he is a holy man?'

The attackers grabbed for more missiles, hurled them. Edmund was temporarily blinded by the deluge of foul yolk, threw up an arm to protect his head. A turnip hit him full in the stomach, bent him double; another glanced off his skull.

'Stop them!' The women shrieked again.

The crowd had swelled, peasants and yeomen alike pushing one another. Somebody shouted, 'Where's the constable?'

A scuffle began; some were trying to drag the young farm labourers away, others were attempting to assist them so that the bombardment of the monk and the beggar could continue.

Amidst the mêlée Nicholas moved with an agility born of practice in such situations; his sly fingers removed money and valuables from purses whilst the wearers were oblivious of everything except the escalating fight. Already Pouk had a bleeding nose and his tall companion was scrapping with a burly tradesmen. A rack of gutted rabbits fell from one of the stalls; a frenzied yapping denoted that the scavenging street curs had scented them.

'*Stop!*'

This time it was not the women who screamed her shrill anger. The tones were deep and commanding. The brawl ceased as quickly as it had begun.

Bill Symes, the constable, had arrived. There was more barking and growling as his hound chased away the street dogs. Men were dusting themselves down, wiping egg yolk from fine doublets and canions.

'There's somebody likely to go to prison afore nightfall!' He stabbed the air with his stick in a threatening fashion. 'Now, what's going on?'

'It's *him*!' Pouk pointed at Edmund who was struggling back up on to his feet. 'The monk tried to stop us pelting the beggar, stood in the way so's he got hit instead.'

'Did you now?' The constable turned on Edmund, wagged a finger, his fleshy features suffused with blood. 'Obstructing the law, eh! I've a good mind to bring you before the churchwarden and have *you* put in the stocks.'

'Let me take the place of the beggar.' It was a genuine plea. 'Free him and I will gladly suffer the humility. Tomorrow as well, if need be. I offer myself for two days for Ned's one. Is that not a fair bargain? And these people can have their fun at my expense.'

'If anything, you'll be in the stocks as well.' It was a half-hearted threat because Symes already had three drunks in the cells. The monk was a nuisance, nothing more. 'Make yourself scarce, brother, before I arrest you. Go on, be off with you and don't let me see you hanging round the stocks again.'

Reluctantly, Edmund turned, made his way through the crowd to a chorus of jeers and cheers.

'Now, let's have no more of this brawling.' Symes turned a fierce expression on the crowd. 'Throw at the beggar peaceably. You've got till nightfall, there's no need to squabble over it.'

'Shame on you, constable, encouraging violence.' The complaining woman's voice was more subdued now. A token protest.

Symes whirled to confront her. 'You go tell that to Martyn Wylde, the churchwarden. See what he has to say, and that goes for any others of you that don't agree with the Poor Laws. Tell 'im, not me. I only do my duty and difficult enough it is with the likes of you lot around.'

Out of the corner of his eye the constable saw Nicholas departing with the furtiveness of a slinking weasel. Doubtless, the trickster had raided a few purses, but this was no time to chase after him. The fellow was fleet of foot; by the time Symes caught up with him the other would doubtless have hidden his ill-gotten gains somewhere.

Bill Symes noted other familiar faces: Benjamin, the wandering pedlar, with the wide brim of his colourful hat pulled down over his face to shade his eyes from the bright sunlight. He was always around on market days. And Robert the Angler, so called because he was known to steal clothes from washing lines with the aid of a fishing rod. So far he, like Nicholas, had eluded arrest by his cunning.

And Gilbert, landlord of the ale house across the way, who had left his bar untended in order to satisfy his curiosity. Some of the area's most substantial tenants, too: Edgar Ridge whose fine garments were covered in dust where he had grappled with a lout and borne him to the floor. Robert Dudley and Victor Gask. And Jane, the whore, who was alluring even in her slovenliness and ragged dress, here to tempt the menfolk to be unfaithful to their wives. She was rumoured to be a witch but that, like Edmund's past, was only hearsay.

It was as if the world and his wife had come to Stratford market.

The constable turned his attention to Ned. The old man hung limply, his head wedged in the neck hole of the stocks. It was impossible to tell whether or not he was unconscious because his eyes were buried beneath a thick layer of congealing egg yolk. In all

17

probability he had passed out. Many of the older ones did at the height of the bombardment.

It mattered not. He would be taken down and thrown into the street at dusk if he was unable to stagger or crawl back to the poor shelter. For the second time that day Symes experienced a feeling that was akin to pity. Perhaps guilt, too. Maybe he was getting too old for the job and it was time a younger man took over.

'Now, let's 'ave no more o' this nonsense!' A parting warning to the packed Market Cross as he accompanied Gilbert back to the ale house. An affray like that made one thirsty, particularly on a hot day.

Bill Symes awoke with a start from a doze, jerked upright in his chair. Be damned, it was dusk already and old Ned was still in the stocks! Still, the churchwarden was less likely to be angry over a late finish than a late start. Wylde had no time for beggars; he conducted a purge akin to that of the Witchfinder on one of the latter's infrequent visits to the town.

'We'd better get up there sharpish, Drake.' Even the dog seemed sluggish tonight. It was a combination of the heat and patrolling the streets for most of the day. Symes knew that he had drunk more than his usual market day quota of ale, for his movements were a little unsteady. Again, he blamed the heat. A good downpour of rain was needed to lay the dust and freshen everything and everybody up.

Alas, the saffron sky was cloudless and a mist hung over the distant Welcombe Hills. There was no hint of rain. Tomorrow would be hot again, perhaps even hotter than today. But the workload would be lighter without the market and the crowds which it attracted.

The streets were almost deserted except for the customary scavenging cats and curs, which even Drake was too tired to chase. Lights from open doorways and windows of ale houses and inns cast a yellow glow in the roadway. Coarse laughter echoed from within. The night was still young.

'Good evening to you, constable.'

Symes started. The tones were like an icy draught in the balmy air and only too recognisable. The dog pressed itself against his leg as if seeking refuge behind his bulk.

'Good evening, churchwarden,' the constable blustered, thinking of petty duties he might have overlooked for which he was about to be reprimanded.

Martyn Wylde was tall and sparse, his sallow complexion seeming almost luminous in the shadow of his broad-brimmed hat. Aquiline features lent an austerity to his stature, his peasecod-bellied doublet like the hooked beak of some gigantic bird of prey in the dusk. His darting eyes missed nothing, seeming to read your very thoughts. A man who moved purposefully and silently, greater men than the constable cringed inwardly at his approach. Many were wishing away the next two months when the time for the election of a successor to Wylde was due, for no churchwarden was permitted to retain his position for more than a year. Wylde would become a yeoman again, no less influential in parish matters but at least stripped of the authority to administer the law with that mercilessness for which he was feared. He would return to being a yeoman farmer. It was predicted in the town that Talbot Christie would be elected churchwarden and he was known to be a fair, if stern, man.

'I have spent the day at the manor.' A pause for effect, a mention of the highest office within the parish. 'I heard on my return that there has been an unseemly brawl at the Market Cross.' Almost an accusation directed at the officer.

'A mere scuffle. I quelled it. There was no harm done, neither damage to property nor injuries to persons. The instigators have been warned of the consequences of a repeat disturbance.'

'And the beggar?'

'I am about to release him now, churchwarden.'

'A pity. The fellow is a pestilence upon our community. Should he be found stealing, in addition to his habitual begging, he must hang. Everybody will benefit from his demise. It is a great pity that one so useless to society has been granted longevity. He is sure to be in his fifties. Worthy men often die much younger.'

'Ned is no thief.'

'Is he not? Rather, you have not been sharp enough to catch him stealing. Watch him, and keep your eyes skinned, tip off your deputies to do likewise, and I warrant we shall have a noose on him before the fall of the leaf.'

'I'll watch him carefully.' Symes made an effort to increase his pace but the other kept in step with him.

'I might as well accompany you to the stocks, constable. I shall be interested to see how the vagrant has fared in the heat of the day. Today has been one of the hottest I can remember and I've seen

19

forty-two summers.'

The deserted Market Cross was sinister in the deep dusk, its spire-like turret and open ground floor reminiscent of a derelict church. The stench of discarded rotted vegetables and eggs hung heavy in the atmosphere.

Ned was still slumped in the stocks; he was unlikely to have had either the guile or the strength to escape, Symes reminded himself. Unless that monk had aided him. He clearly had not.

An undefinable silhouette hanging from the boards, Ned had clearly passed into a state of unconsciousness. Which was predictable, Symes thought.

'Get him out, constable, drag him into the street. If he hasn't the strength to make it to the poor shelter, leave him lying in the gutter.'

The constable struggled to lift the heavy board. His companion made no move to help him for the churchwarden's role was to delegate and to supervise. Silent criticism, urging Symes to hurry, cursing him for his clumsiness.

Ned fell backwards, thumped on to the earthen floor. His body seemed stiff, composed of rheumatic limbs which had become fixed in that enforced posture throughout the daylight hours.

'Drag him out into the street as I instructed you or else we'll have half the vagrants in the district using the market for a shelter.'

The constable did as he was ordered, kicked the dog away for keeping too close to him. The damned hound was getting scared of everybody these days; maybe it was time for a replacement. William, the gamekeeper, would despatch him painlessly with a blast of scattershot.

Ned dragged like a board, ploughed a furrow in the dirt in his wake. His features were plastered with dried mulch. It was impossible to see them.

'Turn him over, constable, so that passers-by don't have to look upon his face.'

As he bent to secure a grip on the inert form, Bill Symes sensed death. It was a feeling born of experience, one of his daily duties was to check the charnel house. You smelled it, an odour that was at once distinguishable from all the other stenches that pervaded the town.

Ned's death was no surprise. The beggar was well past his expected lifespan. At least there would be no pressure to hang him under Wylde's orders. The vagrant's death would be a blessing for all concerned, not least the old man himself who suffered just to survive.

With some difficulty the constable turned the body on to its stomach. As he stood up a shaft of light from the ale house opposite fell on to the ragged form, and Symes gave a grunt of shocked surprise.

There was no doubt that Ned was dead. Between his shoulder blades there was a jagged knife wound.

CHAPTER TWO

The return journey from Stratford to Warwick in one day was an arduous undertaking, particularly when one was getting on in years. It was never a trip to be relished and, consequently, the Reverend Samuel Long was relieved, upon emerging from a strip of woodland, to see the outline of the Welcombe Hills in the distance.

He paused briefly, his tall figure hunched in the saddle, his dark clerical garb and wide-brimmed hat filmed with grey dust. Beneath the heavy clothing he perspired heavily but it would not have been seemly for a man of the Church to have ridden other then fully clad. His eyes were red-rimmed where he had rubbed the dust from them, and his mount was streaked with sweat even though he had not ridden it hard.

He made a mental note to speak to Matthew King, the parish clerk, about the state of the roads. Their condition had worsened since Long had last travelled to Warwick, possibly due to the increase in the number of wheeled vehicles which were using them these days. Potholes and ruts had been gouged out by the iron wheels during the winter when the surface was thick mud; the drought had baked them rock hard, so that on several occasions the parson's horse had stumbled, and once he had almost been thrown.

Saplings were growing on the roadsides. All trees had to be felled close to the main routes between market towns for fear that they might provide cover for lurking highwaymen or footpads. There was a distinct look of negligence about the main highways lately.

Each parish had its own unpaid surveyor of roads; King was responsible for the route from Stratford to the point where it met the Warwick boundary. For eight hours on four consecutive days each month, two labourers with oxen, horses and carts had to be provided for road maintenance. Clearly, this procedure had lapsed. The parson would lodge a complaint on behalf of the Church; if King did not order the work to be done immediately, then Long would speak to the churchwarden about it. If that did not have the desired effect, he would send a letter to the bishop. The bishop was influential, respected even by the Lord Lieutenant, for the Church was still all powerful in spite of the Queen's relaxation of some of her predecessor's inflexible diktats. One way or another, travel between Stratford and Warwick would be made safer and more comfortable.

The Reverend Long turned, glanced behind him. The wood through which he had just ridden was dark and forbidding with the approach of nightfall. Shadows, twisted oaks with giant boles, took on shapes a thousand times more fearsome than that of a waiting robber, became things that had no place upon God's earth.

There were rumours, too, according to the constable, that Edward Las, the notorious highwayman, had been seen in the area. Of course, you could not believe everything that Symes told you; he was given to fanciful stories in an attempt to inflate his own ego and enhance his reputation, especially after a round of the ale houses. The harassment of beggars and gypsies paled into insignificance and he was exonerated by those whose sympathies lay with the poor if it was known that he was on the look out for a dangerous highwayman.

But even highwaymen were preferable to some of the evils that were lurking within the parish right now.

Long's fears stemmed from the meeting to which he had been summoned that day at the Lord Lieutenant's residence, a gathering of clergy which had been drawn from far and wide throughout the county. The bishop himself had been present, which only emphasised the urgency of the seminar.

A trumpeter and herald, the steward presiding as speaker; there had even been a Jury of Tenants to support the motion in this mini-parliament. Richard ap Cynon, Lord Lieutenant of Warwickshire, had gone to great lengths to instil into all those present that the meeting was in no way routine. Informality bred apathy; pomp and ceremony underlined a crisis. And most certainly the county had a crisis.

For witchcraft, an insidious ever-present scourge upon God-fearing communities, was upon Warwickshire like a plague. Luke Jeffries, the Witchfinder, had been sent for. A messenger had already been despatched to Derbyshire where the infamous hunter of all who dabbled in the works of the devil was purported to be conducting a purge on the enemies of Christianity.

It was a worrying, nay *terrifying*, revelation. The bishop had gone into detail concerning some of the evil practices carried out by witches. His audience had trembled at his words, closed their eyes and prayed for the salvation of their congregations. And for themselves. Even Richard ap Cynon's ruddy complexion had looked a shade paler, Long thought, at the end of the bishop's address.

'Satan is amongst us, none of us are invincible to his guile. Our very souls are in danger of being cast into everlasting torment if we do not rid our parishes of his disciples.'

Long's fingers trembled on the reins, and he kicked the flanks of his mount. Reluctantly, the horse eased forward, its only incentive to complete the long, hard journey the thought of the water trough at the parsonage. All the wayside puddles had long dried up.

It would be full dark by the time the parson arrived back in town. The deepening dusk only served to recall the bishop's words, the way his voice had quavered lightly at the mention of some of the obscenities conducted by those who had forsaken God for the devil and all his works.

Parson Long's thoughts turned to Jane, the whore. Folks said that she was a witch, whispered it in awe. He had dismissed it as malicious gossip by wives whose husbands had strayed into her grubby bed. In the gathering darkness it seemed a possibility, for oft times she had been fined for her absence from church on the Sabbath. It was as though the place held a fear for her, as if her enforced attendances caused her anguish. And that, in itself, was a sign of guilt.

The Reverend Samuel Long was also apprehensive about the coming of the Witchfinder. Unquestionably, Satan must be vanquished, but sometimes Long felt that all Jeffries was interested in was a scapegoat, a confession for the records, his own personal tally of successful purges. An instance sprang to mind: old Beth who had lived in the poor shelter for the last decade and would surely not have survived last winter. She hadn't, because the Witchfinder had condemned her to the ducking stool and she had drowned. Her untimely death was surely a sign of her innocence and yet, according to those who had examined the hag, she bore the devil's mark on her bony buttocks, the obscene kiss in the shape of a cloven hoof, and that was proof, according to Jeffries, that she had, at some time, communed with Satan. Even if she was not an active disciple at the time when she was condemned, she had, at some stage, practised satanic rites, and that warranted her being put to death. And, did she not have an affinity with the stray cats that roamed the streets? And, furthermore, had not people witnessed her collecting hemlock?

Long was not convinced, yet both the Lord Lieutenant and the bishop gave their blessing to a purge of witches. Who was he, a mere parson and a humble servant of the Almighty, to question their wisdom? All the same, he feared the coming of the Witchfinder. It heralded suffering and death, torture and execution.

It was almost dark as he rode past the Guild Chapel. His intention was to ride straight on to the parsonage but the church, mirrored in the water of a reed-fringed river, seemed to call him, its tranquillity in stark contrast to his troubled musings.

He pulled his mount over, though it made a token resistance for its thoughts were on the stone trough outside its stable. A waft of cool air from the Avon was momentarily refreshing. Long hesitated, tempted by the prospect of the cooling drink and sustenance which his housekeeper would have prepared in readiness for his homecoming. He fought off the temptation: Satan's erosion of one's faith began in trivial ways such as this. Eat and drink, put physical needs before spiritual ones.

He needed to pray tonight, to thank God for his safe journey, to ask that the innocent might be spared from the Witchfinder. He often went into the church after dark, he needed no light to find his way to the altar steps, Just to kneel and wait for God to speak to him. It was an experience which gave him peace of mind, a reassurance. A refuge from the harsh realities of the world in which he lived.

He tethered the horse, fumbled in the pouch strapped to the belt around his waist for the door key. Had he had his way, the church would have been left permanently unlocked, for, surely, it was there for the people to enter and pray in whenever they felt the need. But Lord Armdale had ruled that it must be kept locked at nights and when the parson was away on parish affairs, for fear that vagrants might use it for shelter. And what harm if they did? Were the homeless not God's children, also? The churchwarden argued that valuable artefacts might be stolen by robbers. If folks felt the need for prayers apart from on the Sabbath, then they could pray in their homes, in the fields, wherever, for God would always listen to them.

Why then, Long argued privately, was it necessary to compel everybody over the age of six years to attend church on Sundays? Absence, without a valid reason, such as illness, resulted in a fine. Parishioners should be encouraged to attend services because it was their wish, not for fear of punishment if they stayed away. But he dared not voice his views, for they would probably have resulted in excommunication. Possibly that was why Edmund had been expelled from his monastery – at least Long liked to think that it might have been for such a reason.

The night breeze wafted again, this time bringing with it the stench of death from the charnel house which adjoined the chancel. There were always corpses awaiting burial; at times the gravediggers could not keep pace with the death rate. In winter it wasn't so bad but in summer the unburied decomposed rapidly and smelled. But death was part of life.

The tethered horse whinnied, and its restlessness brought a sense of unease to the parson. Perhaps it was the smell of death, or maybe the animal thirsted. Like himself. But God was more important than physical discomfort.

Something was wrong. He hesitated, the key outstretched between a clammy forefinger and thumb. A kind of premonition. No, he was just tired. The trauma of the day, the dire warnings of witches in their midst, was playing on his mind.

It was full dark in the shadow of the church.

Long did not need to fumble for the keyhole. A quarter of a century of unlocking that door enabled him to find it unerringly.

Except tonight.

The heavy key met with no aperture, no scraping as it slotted into place awaiting a clockwise turn. He tensed, thought that perhaps he had stopped a couple of paces short of the door, that in his exhaustion he had misjudged the distance.

He stepped forward, thrust with his extended hand again.

Still there was nothing, just a void that was blacker than the night itself, exuding a chill that had his heated flesh suddenly goosebumping.

Only then did he realise that the church door was already wide open.

He grunted his surprise. There had to be a perfectly ordinary reason for Holy Trinity's being unlocked. Perhaps someone had need to pray – the suddenly bereaved, for example – and they had gone in search of the parish clerk who carried a duplicate key. On occasions a sobbing widow or mother had sought out himself and he had willingly escorted them to the church, prayed with them and then left them in God's presence, returning later to lock the building.

There might be some poor soul praying at the altar now. He resisted the temptation to call out for fear of disturbing them.

There was nobody inside the church.

The Reverend Long knew, without any doubt, that whoever had been and unlocked the door was now gone. He sensed the emptiness, it came at him with a rush of cold air from within which had that initial prickling travelling up from the nape of his neck into his scalp. His premonition returned. There was something dreadfully amiss.

He stumbled in through the open door, bumped against a pew in his haste. There were candles placed in readiness on the stone window ledges. He groped for them, ran his fingers along the shelf; there were no ornate silver candlesticks. He touched something — the feel of smooth wax told him that it was a candle fallen from its holder.

He held it with shaking fingers, waited whilst the flame burned, cast its radius of flickering, wan light. Shadows, grotesque shapes that might have come straight from that dark forest on the outskirts of town, creatures of the night that mocked him, darted back and changed form; lurked beyond the light, whispered amongst themselves, came at him again in different form.

'Begone, vain phantasms, for this is the house of God where none shall harm those who have faith!' He called out at them in a croaking voice, saw how they retreated.

The wick flared and now he saw where previously there had been only darkness. His cry of anguish and terror came out as a strangled hiss, and he clutched at a stone pillar to prevent himself from falling. His vision swam; he prayed that he might be mistaken, that what he saw was but some nightmarish mirage brought on by heat and exhaustion.

He tried to disbelieve but in the end he believed, accepted the awfulness of what he saw in the dancing candlelight. He offered up an apology to God on behalf of whoever had done this, but there was no answer. It was as if the Almighty had deserted this scene of obscene violation.

The altar was smashed into a heap of kindling, the fine velvet cloth shredded and draped over the wreckage. Gone were the artefacts, the silver communion plates and the vessel of consecrated wine.

26

There was no sign of the heavy gold crucifix presented to Holy Trinity by Queen Elizabeth upon her ascension to the throne. Only the original oaken one that hung on the wall above remained, and when he saw this the parson gave a cry of terror.

For it hung upside down, a symbol of Lucifer against which the bishop had warned only that afternoon.

The Reverend Samuel Long coughed in the tallow fumes, instinctively backed away. All around him was a scene of desecration, an outright denial of God. A stained glass window depicting the crucifixion had been smashed, the stone font had been overturned. The pulpit from which he had preached countless sermons had been torn down like a sapling in a winter gale, just a jagged stump remaining. A statue of the Virgin Mary had been obscenely defaced. He closed his eyes, dared look no more.

A draught extinguished the candle, plunged him into blackness, clutching a smoking wick in his shaking hand. It seemed that the temperature had plummeted to a January iciness, snowy winds gusting in through the open door and broken window.

Hands reached out for him, freezing fingers stroked at his features. He turned to flee, banged against a pew, scarcely noticed the pain. Those awful shadowy shapes had substance now, he sensed them all around him. Creatures that had been freed from the torments of hell, bent on revenge against those who had chosen to keep faith with God when Satan was cast from the heavens.

Now Satan had returned, brought with him his obscene disciples to overthrow Christianity and establish his own domain of evil upon the earth.

Outside, the horse neighed, reared, snapped free of its tether and vanished into the night with a thundering of hooves, fled the evil which had spawned within this once holy place. And the parson staggered into the street, stumbling after it, crying out a warning to any who might hear him that the devil was in their midst.

CHAPTER THREE

'He's been stabbed.' The constable straightened up, his normally ruddy features pale in the glow from the alehouse lights. 'Somebody has *murdered* old Ned!'

The churchwarden bent forward, sucked on pouted lips, a habit of his on the rare occasions when a suitable expletive eluded him.

He nodded his agreement. There was no denying that Bill Symes spoke the truth, the jagged wound in the emaciated back of the vagrant's corpse was proof in itself. The blood had congealed; doubtless there was a pool of it behind the stocks but it would have passed unnoticed in the mulch of missiles that had been hurled at the prisoner throughout the day.

'A hunting knife, doubtless.' Wylde's voice was a whispered hiss. The blade had gone in deep, had twisted and gouged as force had been exerted to withdraw it. The rotting garment had ripped and shredded, exposing the fatal mutilation.

'Who would want to kill an old beggar?' The constable's tone was almost a plea to his companion to provide the answer to his question. 'And *why*?'

Martyn Wylde shook his head in perplexity. The only people wishing death upon the beggars were those who upheld the law in the parish. And they would do it legitimately. By hanging, provided theft or some other crime could be reasonably proved. Otherwise they hoped that the unfortunate would die from stress in the stocks and cease to be a burden upon parish taxes.

If you murdered, you risked the gallows and no vagrant was worth hanging for. All of which he pointed out to the officer to save himself a barrage of questions.

'Well, somebody done it.' Symes ran his tongue along his thick lips which had suddenly gone dry. He glanced quickly in the direction of the ale house.

'An astute observation on your part, constable.' Wylde laughed humourlessly. 'Ned most certainly did not commit suicide; even were

28

he a contortionist, his hands were secured. As you rightly say, we must assume that somebody killed him for a reason unknown to us.'

'We can't leave him lyin' in the gutter now, sir.'

'Unfortunately not.' Wylde eyed a couple of roaming curs. Only his companion's dog had them keeping their distance. Left unattended, the human corpse would soon have been scavenged. Even stinking beggar flesh was appetising to starving canines. 'You'd best get a couple of your assistants to drive the cart down from the charnel house.'

'Yes, sir.'

'And accompany them, constable, ensure that the job is done quickly and efficiently. Disease can spread swiftly in hot weather if bodies are left lying around. Which reminds me, exhort the gravediggers to greater alacrity. There are already four bodies in the charnel house awaiting paupers' burials. See that they are all buried tomorrow. Ned, too.'

'Yes, churchwarden.' Symes was uneasy. 'But 'adn't we. . . well, I mean, the old fellow's been murdered and all murders 'ave to be investigated. . .'

'Of course the murder will be investigated.' There was a sharpness in the churchwarden's voice at the very suggestion that the taking of a human life might go unprobed. 'He who takes a life, forfeits his own life, constable. You must begin enquiries right away.'

Symes nodded. It wouldn't be easy. There had been hundreds of folks milling in the market place today; it could be any one of them. Maybe some yeoman or tenant farmer with a grudge against vagrants that had become an obsession.

'Those youths, Pouk and his friends' – a sudden thought that might stand him in good stead with the churchwarden. 'They started a fight. The murder could have been done then.'

'A possibility, constable. Question them. and if you are in any doubt, arrest them and have them brought before the justices of the peace. Rabble, no better than vagrants.'

'And Edmund, the monk, 'e was causin' trouble, tried to stop them throwing at Ned.'

'Unlikely, but speak to him. He is against violence and suffering, it is unlikely to be him.'

'Nicholas and Robert the Angler were hanging around, too.'

Wylde hissed his impatience, half turned away. 'Constable.' He spoke slowly, deliberately, the way he always did when his wrath was stirring; he was not one to tolerate fools gladly, and Constable

Symes was a classic fool, in a scarlet and black uniform, whose only redeeming feature was that he obeyed orders. Most of the time, anyway. 'Constable, there are many people to be questioned. Deliberate upon the faces you saw around the Market Cross today. Speak with each and every one of them, ask them, too, whom they saw there. We must be seen to be trying to catch the murderer. Lord Armdale, like the Lord Lieutenant himself, is known to have an underlying sympathy for the poor. But the Poor Laws, instigated by Her Majesty, demand that beggars be expatriated, sturdy ones flogged or put in the stocks. Ned would not have been committed to the stocks except that his begging was persistent; a younger man would have been flogged. Had he died under the stress of his punishment, the matter would have gone no further. But somebody, for some unknown reason, murdered him and thus we have to make every effort to bring the killer to the gallows. We cannot risk alienating the lower echelons of our society by taking no action. I doubt whether we shall find the murderer but at least we will have done our best. Do you understand what I say?'

'Yes, churchwarden,' Symes's head drooped in obedience.

'And, constable?'

'Sir?'

'Do not forget the Romanies camped out in the forest. Gypsies are rogues, not to be trusted. Have you seen any in town today?'

'A couple, sir, but they weren't doin' no harm.'

'One rarely sees a gypsy committing a felony. They are both furtive and cunning. At least use this business as an excuse to visit their encampment and warn them to move on.'

'I'll go first thing after daylight, sir.'

'Good, and just one more thing, constable.'

Symes tensed, seemed to flinch. The dog was back at his heel, cringing.

'You remember that business of the murdered peasant woman two springs ago, don't you, Symes?'

'Indeed, I do, sir.' It had been the scandal of the parish, a farm labourer's daughter found in a roadside ditch with her throat slit; she had bled like a stuck Michaelmas goose. Folks had said it was the moonmen who had stayed overnight in one of the barns who had murdered the woman when she stumbled upon their poultry thieving. They were nowhere to be seen at first light, and all that remained of the farmer's barnyard roosters was a mass of feathers. Symes and three armed constables had trailed the men as far as the

Worcestershire border but the fugitives had been too swift for their pursuers. A week later a tenant farmer's wife had been arrested, charged with murder and found guilty. She had hanged. Her husband had found primitive pleasure in the unwashed flesh of a peasant wench, the wife had discovered his illicit affair and had killed the girl in a frenzy of jealous rage.

'And it was not you who apprehended her murderer, Symes.' There was no mistaking the churchwarden's tone of reproach. 'The constabulary jumped to conclusions, opted for the obvious, didn't they?'

The other nodded, refrained from adding that it was the churchwarden himself who had suggested that the moonmen should be caught and questioned. Symes and his deputies had saddled up forthwith.

'As a result,' a sharp pause, 'the Lord Lieutenant sent in his own jack-in-office to investigate. There wasn't a cranny in town into which he didn't poke his nose. He even found the Swan ale wanting; the landlord had been diluting it. Samuel Train was churchwarden that year, and his position came under threat because he had failed in the checking of the ale. So we don't want the county sending in Kent again, do we, constable? Having the fellow living close to the town is bad enough in itself, but if he was commissioned to find the murderer in an official capacity, we don't know what he might unearth. Even *you* might lose your job, Symes. Who knows what minor misdemeanours you have been committing without my knowledge? And I should be in trouble for failing to detect your petty roguery.'

'I 'aven't been doing' nothin', sir.' The constable swallowed, his Adam's apple bobbing up and down. 'I swear it.' Every constable took the odd small bribe from tradesmen in return for overlooking small market irregularities. It was an accepted practice, the churchwarden was well aware of it; often the bribes given to himself were somewhat larger.

'Of course not.' Wylde smiled, a stretching of his thin lips. 'But the fact remains, we don't want Kent sniffing through the town. I doubt that a beggar's murder will carry much significance,' his tone lacked conviction, 'but at least be seen to be doing something to find the murderer, constable. That, in itself, may well satisfy Lord Armdale, and the Lord Lieutenant, even, should it reach his ears. Now, get this corpse removed to the charnel house before anybody else sees it and—'

'Somebody's coming, churchwarden!'

The constable was alerted by the way the hound had come erect, its hackles raised, muzzle pointed towards the dimly lit street, a low growl in its throat. Martyn Wylde whirled in a half-crouch. The approaching footsteps were fast and dragging, denoted urgency. The wheezing breaths were those of somebody in fear.

'It's the *parson!*'

The Reverend Samuel Long was recognisable only by his travel-stained clerical raiment; his hat was gone, his shoulder-length grey hair was matted with sweat and dust. His bony hands clawed the air as if he swatted troublesome gnats on a warm evening.

He came stumbling out of the darkness, a cadaver arisen from the charnel house, spittle frothing on his bloodless lips, his cries of terror reduced to a gurgling in his scrawny throat. At one point he almost collapsed but the sight of the constable and the churchwarden seemed to give him an extra strength, enough to reach them, to grasp Symes's arm for support.

The dog's growl became a whine; its tail curled beneath its lice-ridden body. Again, it sensed terror.

'Reverend, what has happened?' Wylde saw the other's eyes, the way they glanced heavenwards, rolled.

'God protect us,' Long gasped, would surely have fallen this time had not the others grabbed him. His head turned as he shied from the shadows. He might have screamed, but it came out as a croak.

'*Satan is amongst us!*'

'I am inclined to agree with you, Reverend.' Wylde cast a half-glance towards the corpse in the gutter.

'He has taken the church for his own vile temple, desecrated it beyond belief.'

It was the heat, of course, the churchwarden decided. That, and the parson's age. He had progressed faster towards senility than even Ned the Beggar.

'*I tell you, the church is desecrated! Valuable artefacts have been stolen!*'

Wylde stiffened, looked at the constable. 'Another job for you, Symes, *after* you've removed the—'

'We must notify Lord Armdale, send a messenger to Warwick. The Lord Lieutenant and the bishop must be informed that Satan is in Stratford. Let us thank the Lord that the Witchfinder has already been summoned.'

'Jeffries?' Wylde's fingers tightened on the cleric's arm, and the other gasped at the pressure. 'Who has sent for Luke Jeffries?'

'The. . . the bishop.' Long mouthed a frightened whisper. 'He warned us and his prophecy has come true faster than even his grace thought. Churchwarden, constable, Holy Trinity has been robbed, the devil himself has entered and defiled God's house. I beg of you to come at once.'

Martyn Wylde looked at the still form lying in the roadside. Another hour or two would make little difference to Ned, nor to the townspeople. Any who saw him at this hour would be too drunk to remember; far better that folks were told by the constable than that they saw for themselves and spread wild rumours. Doubtless Satan would be blamed by the superstitious for the old man's death.

'We'd better get down to the church,' Wylde said to his companions. His features were in shadow or else they might have seen how his complexion had paled to the whiteness of a corpse. Martyn Wylde had a healthy respect for the devil, but he could have counted on the long bony fingers of one hand the number of mortals whom he secretly feared. Amongst those was Luke Jeffries.

For everybody, regardless of their status, had a lurking terror of the Witchfinder. His authority came directly from the Privy Council, and it was a brave, and foolish, justice of the peace who dared to question Luke Jeffries's evidence. The finger of suspicion might point at any one of them, and when it did, a confession was a foregone conclusion.

The Witchfinder, like the plague, left death and suffering in his wake wherever he travelled.

CHAPTER FOUR

Guy Kent might have been taken for an apprentice archer by those who did not know him, and there were many, for it was preferable that an informant of the Lord Lieutenant travelled incognito whenever and wherever possible. He wore green because it was his favourite colour, for no other reason. His headgear was of the kind worn by bowmen, of velvet and with a narrow brim. His doublet and tight-fitting canions accentuated his slender stature. His bright yellow nether socks were in dazzling contrast to the rest of his attire.

His fair love-locks belied his thirty years, as did his choice to go clean shaven when most men of his age sported a beard with pride. He had, though, given a solemn vow to his lover, Diana Hawker, that, upon her consent to marriage, he would snip off his locks and allow his facial hair to grow unchecked. Possibly this threat was why she still refused the ties of matrimony.

He might even have made it for that very reason, for he still valued his freedom.

His clean-cut features and clear blue eyes had a look of naivety about them, a youthfulness, something else which he played to his advantage. Strangers underestimated him, dismissed him as inconsequential. Often they were careless with their talk within earshot. Guy Kent's boyishness was his forte.

All of which was why Richard ap Cynon, Lord Lieutenant of Warwickshire, had chosen him for a role which was not officially recognised within the appointments of his local government. He overlooked the fact that Kent's breath sometimes smelled of tobacco. Every man was entitled to one small vice. His own was of a liquid nature.

'Somebody has murdered an old beggar in the stocks at Stratford.' The Lord Lieutenant's expression was inscrutable, those dark eyes which so often flashed with sudden anger gave no hint of his inner feelings. He spoke almost casually, looked for a reaction.

'Who would want to kill a beggar, my lord, except by execution, and then only if he has committed an offence punishable by death?' The reply was evasive, a duel of wits and words.

Richard ap Cynon's long dark hair, groomed to perfection, swirled as he turned to look out of the window across the rolling parkland. His fine lace-edged coat, his height and poise, his pointed beard, had a swashbuckling effect. His age was indeterminable but Kent thought the other was barely more than a couple of years older than himself. A hard but fair man, you either liked or disliked him; there was no room for compromise.

For some moments there was silence, then, without turning round, the Lord Lieutenant spoke. 'Two questions I would give a ransom to know the answers to, Kent. Who and why. The Poor Laws have brought untold suffering, worse even than before. A beggar has died, one amongst dozens in Stratford. Neither mourned nor missed, he would probably have died soon, anyway. So,' his shoulders shrugged in mock contempt, 'why do we concern ourselves? I cannot give a truthful answer except that I feel there is more to this man's death than meets the eye. At the moment the constable is making enquiries on the orders of the churchwarden, but I fear it will only be a token effort. There is only one man capable of getting to the bottom of this business.' He whirled round suddenly and only Kent's iron resolve prevented him from flinching from the flashing dark eyes that focused on him. 'You are the man for the job, Kent.'

'You wish me to begin an investigation, sir?'

'I hesitate.' The tall man demonstrated a rare moment of indecision, stroked his beard thoughtfully. 'Perhaps it would be better to wait until I have the churchwarden's report. On the other hand, I know that the findings will be inconclusive, and perhaps to wait would be a mistake. With every passing hour the trail grows colder. And yet, sending you into your home town on official business could be equally mistaken.'

Kent waited patiently as the other struggled with his dilemma. Only too well the 'Eyes and Ears of the Lord Lieutenant', as some of the townspeople dubbed him, recognised the truth of the old adage that familiarity bred contempt. Nobody would offer information willingly, some would shun him, others would go out of their way to obstruct him, a man who ran with both the deer and the hunters. After the last occasion, public sympathy was divided between the slain peasant wench and the murderess; a woman scorned had acted in a moment of passion, a young girl had been the victim of a seduction, tempted by material gains which otherwise would never have been within her reach. Both women were dead: without Kent's interference the one would not have gone to the gallows and better for all concerned if she had not. They would not trust him.

'One day things will change.' Richard ap Cynon was staring out of the window again. 'The homeless will be afforded a better standard of living. But they and their offspring, for generations hence, will always be peasantry. The rich and the poor have to learn to live side by side in harmony. The Poor Laws, and their harsh extirpation of vagrants, are creating a division that will smoulder for all time, a division of the classes. The Peasants' Revolt in the fourteenth century has not been forgotten, nor the promises that were made and broken. I sense that it could happen again in our own time.

Ned's murder might already have lit the fuse, who knows? Which is why we have to find out who killed him, and why. So, against my better judgement, Kent, I shall send you to Stratford. It may well be the hardest task I have so far commissioned from you. And the most dangerous, for he who plunges a dagger into the back of a harmless old man will not hesitate to murder a hound of justice who has picked up his scent.'

'I shall be alert at all times, my lord.' Kent sensed a dryness in his mouth, which might have been caused by the occasional use of tobacco.

'One other thing.' The Lord Lieutenant's expression was strained. 'Doubtless you have heard of other disturbing events that have taken place within the town?'

'The church has been violated. I heard the news on my way here.'

'There is a resurgence of witchcraft. The seminar which we held here two days ago was obviously too late to prevent such an act against the Almighty. The Witchfinder is on his way to Stratford, in all probability has already arrived, for such a serious act against God needs immediate retribution. No town likes a witch hunt, even when Satan is in their midst. This will make your mission doubly difficult, but I must order you to treat the murder as a separate issue. Do not allow yourself to be distracted by witches or those who seek them out.'

'I shall let others go about their business whilst I go about mine.' Kent rose to his feet, sensing that his audience was at an end.

'Good.' The Lord Lieutenant smiled. 'But we must not overlook the faint possibility that the beggar's death had an involvement with witchcraft, might be a human sacrifice. But I ask you merely to bear this in mind, not to pursue it. If perchance your enquiries lead you down that dark and dangerous path, then inform me at once. Under no circumstances confide in Luke Jeffries, neither help nor hinder him, for any liaison could have serious consequences. He is a law unto himself, answerable only to the Privy Council, and even I could not save you were you to fall foul of him. Do I make myself understood?'

'Absolutely.' Kent's mouth was very dry now and he knew that it had nothing to do with the new fashion of smoking tobacco. 'I shall ride for Stratford at once.'

As Guy Kent rode south, he noticed that in the far distance the sky had darkened, thought that he detected a faint rumble of thunder. The storm clouds were already gathering over Stratford, as though the Almighty was seeking retribution for Satan's act against Him.

Or else the heavens themselves were rebelling at the coming of the Witchfinder.

CHAPTER FIVE

'The corpse was buried yesterday.' Martyn Wylde failed to disguise the slight edge of smugness in his tone. 'Even a pauper's grave requires an exhumation order from the Privy Council before it can be touched.'

Kent nodded. His blue eyes did not betray his momentary sense of frustration; he had expected as much. 'I don't think I would have gained much by examining it. Stab wounds are much the same wherever you find them. It was just a thought, a starting point.'

'I assure you, Kent,' the churchwarden reclined in the carved wooden chair which he referred to as his 'seat of office', placed his fingertips together and adopted a pensive mood, 'Constable Symes has questioned dozens of people, maybe even a hundred. Nobody noticed anything amiss. There was a scuffle between some youths and some sympathisers; the killing could well have happened then. As for who did it, and the motive, your notion is as good as mine. But if there is anything I can do to help,' his eyes narrowed, their expression making a lie out of his words, 'please do not hesitate to request my assistance. Of course, I am extremely busy at present.' He rose to his feet. 'Much of my time is devoted to the Witchfinder.'

Kent refrained from enquiring how Luke Jeffries was faring; nobody was told until they were hauled from their homes and interrogated. The methods used to extract a confession from a suspected witch were told in hushed whispers throughout the county. Few had lived to recount their tortures.

'Naturally, I shall need to talk to people, some of whom have already questioned by Constable Symes.' The envoy's eyes were chips of blue ice now, challenging the other to defy the orders of the Lord Lieutenant if he dared.

'Of course.' A sweep of a hand that indicated the doorway. 'Now, if you will excuse me. . .'

Kent stepped out of the town hall into Chapel Street, shaded his eyes against the brightness of the midday sun. The street was unusually deserted: a couple of mangy curs were fighting over a whitened bone, an old woman was hurrying along with a disturbing sense of urgency, not even pausing when she stumbled on the uneven cobblestones and dislodged a couple of eggs from the basket on her arm. She glanced from side to side as she went, and even from that distance there was no mistaking the fear on her wizened features.

A rumble of wagon wheels from further down attracted his attention. A covered cart hove into view, slowed as it approached the chancel of the Holy Trinity church. Kent shaded his eyes, watched two men unload something from the rear. Another body had been delivered to the charnel house.

He wondered idly how the unfortunate had died.

'The gypsies are edgy.' Diana Hawker spoke with her back to Guy Kent as she busily chopped herbs on a board at the table. 'I was in the woods today gathering wild garlic and I chanced upon their encampment. Some of the caravans were loaded up – they'll be gone by morning.'

'The Witchfinder knows no boundaries.' Kent toyed with an empty clay pipe, resisted the temptation to smoke; later, perhaps, and out of doors, for the fair-haired girl busily preparing a herb salad for their evening meal strongly disapproved of his latest habit.

'If the Lord had intended us to smoke,' she had told him repeatedly, 'then He would have provided us with chimneys on our heads.'

Which, he supposed, was logical.

Diana was the daughter of a Staffordshire landowner. A few years ago an outbreak of plague had wiped out the family with the exception of her brother and herself. Not wishing to remain in her inherited home with her brother and his new bride, she had accepted a generous payment from him and headed into the adjacent county.

The money had enabled her to purchase this delightful thatched cottage at Newbold-on-Stour, nestling snugly in the shelter of an oak wood and with almost an acre of land. From late childhood she had shown an interest in herbal remedies and, much to the chagrin of the physicians in Stratford, she had cultivated her land, grown numerous herbs, and had already earned herself a reputation for the preparation of medicines. Her allowance had enabled her to sell more cheaply than her rivals and her remedies were affordable to the poor.

The parish, out to protect their own kind, had increased her taxes. On more than one occasion Matthew King had called to inspect her ledgers; he had not, on his first visit, expected to find a neat and accurate set of figures written with a quill that might have rivalled the bard himself. He failed to find fault but, nevertheless, imposed an increased taxation.

Kent's arrival caused malicious gossip amongst the townspeople; the parson protested to the bishop but Guy was in the employ of the Lord Lieutenant, and if Richard ap Cynon made no move to discipline his servant then the relationship was obviously accepted, if not approved.

The law demanded that both Guy and Diana attended church on Sundays; co-habitation without marriage was not a reason for excommunication. Their absence would have been punished with a fine. The scandal died down but it was not forgotten. Whenever Diana rode into town, passers-by eyed her slyly with more than a casual interest, looked for a swelling in her belly. When she was with child, as surely she must be before long, then the tongues would wag again. In secret, of course.

'Symes appears to have questioned most of the townspeople as well as those who came into market from outlying districts,' Guy said thoughtfully. 'In his own way, of course. Maybe somebody told him something that hasn't registered – the fellow is decidedly dull. A good man when it comes to arresting drunks and vagrants, helped by that dog of his, of course, but his talents stop there. Apparently, he attempted a bier rite; several of the vagrants attended Ned's burial and the constable was watching carefully in case the corpse started to bleed in the presence of the murderer. Superstition, I fear, will not reveal the killer to us.'

'Perhaps it was just a drunken killing.' Diana did not sound convincing. 'There are numerous alehouse murders over the years. A market place mêlée, somebody draws a knife, plunges it into the nearest person who, in this case, happens to be Ned the Beggar. Nobody notices, and realising what he has done – or perhaps not even realising it in his drunken stupor – the murderer slips away and there is no chance of catching him. That might be all there is to it.'

'I think not. Just a feeling I have. The problem is knowing where to start. Most of the regular itinerants have vacated the town, fled from the Witchfinder. Edmund is living in a cave at Guy's Cliff, Nicholas is occupying a ruined barn at Crimscote, and nobody knows where Robert the Angler is. The parson is confined to his bed. It was feared that he had had a stroke, but it appears to be just shock and exhaustion.'

Diana heaped a mixture of chopped herbs on to a platter, passed it to him. 'Here, at least this will fortify you.' She bent forward, kissed him. 'Ugh, you've been smoking again. I can smell it on your breath.'

He smiled. 'The garlic will mask the odour.'

'But it will not destroy the harmful effects of the weed!' She wagged a finger. 'It is said that when Raleigh was seen smoking, somebody threw a pitcher of water over him.'

'Folklore,' he laughed. 'If the story is true, it is because they presumed him to have caught fire. Nobody has protested about the eating of potatoes except for the price. A delicacy of the rich. Tobacco is relatively cheap by comparison.'

'And what pleasure is there in sucking smoke into your mouth and puffing it out again?'

'A cold man's fire, a hungry man's food, a lonely man's friend.' He laughed at his own recitation.

'You are not cold, you have food on your plate,' her fingers touched him lightly, 'and you have me. All that comes between us is your infernal tobacco smoking.'

'It aids my powers of concentration,' he chewed thoughtfully, 'and at the moment I am short of inspiration. Ned was killed for a reason, and when I discover that reason it will lead me to his murderer. First, I must plod in the footsteps of our well-meaning constable, speak to those with whom he has spoken. Then. . .'

'What then?'

'That is when I shall need an inspiration. At the moment, even with the assistance of tobacco, it eludes me.'

'Good morning, Nicholas, I see that you have had a good haul recently. From the market, I presume?'

Nicholas leaped up in alarm, his reactions as sharp as the ornately handled knife which he had in his hand. An assortment of trinkets scattered as his feet caught them, coins clinked and rolled. An oath came from his thin lips, and there was a glimmer of fear in his closely set eyes.

'Sir, you startled me. I did not hear your approach.'

Kent smiled. He had gone to great lengths to ensure that his approach might go undetected, making a wide detour of the ruined barn in order to utilise every scrap of available cover. His gaze flicked over the other. In spite of his makeshift temporary home, Nicholas's appearance was immaculate. He might for all the world have come straight from the tailor's: his piccadills had almost a newness about them, he was shaved and washed and his hair was groomed to perfection. A thief, a confidence trickster, he might have passed for the son of a gentleman. Which was all part of his façade; when he was not thieving, he was persuading gullible people to part with their money on some slender pretext.

'I am a pedlar, sir, I ply my trade at the market as well as selling on the streets.'

'Possibly Benjamin, the wandering pedlar, is missing a few of these.' Kent stooped, picked up a mirror and some gloves, eyed the scattered coins with undisguised suspicion. 'Or one of Benjamin's customers.'

'No!' Nicholas's denial was vehement; he swallowed. 'I assure you, sir, the money is the proceeds of legitimate trading, the wares I pick up for resale from passing gypsies.'

'I shall be talking to the Romanies in the woods of the Welcombe Hills later.' Kent tossed the items back on to the floor. The other had gone to considerable trouble to make this tumbledown building habitable. He had used some old boards as draught prevention, the floor had been swept clean. There was some bedding in the corner, neatly rearranged after a night's sleep. Overall, the surroundings did not give the impression of those of a man on the move.

'I purchased them from some gypsies outside Leamington,' Nicholas added just too hastily, averting his eyes. 'A week, maybe ten days, ago.'

'A man could hang for theft,' Kent spoke casually, saw how his quarry swallowed again, blanched.

'Sir, I assure you, I am no thief.'

'A trickster is a thief, it is just that he employs a different method of obtaining his ill-gotten gains.'

Nicholas was decidedly uneasy, which was how Kent wanted him.

'I have little time to concern myself with common thieves and tricksters,' he smiled. 'Do you know Ned the Beggar?'

The sudden question seemed to jerk the coney-catcher, who trembled visibly. 'Everybody, whether they live in Stratford or are

41

merely passing through, is familiar with Ned. I hear he is dead.'
Nicholas's lower lip quavered slightly.

'Aye, he is dead. *Murdered.*'

'But nobody would want to—'

'*Somebody* obviously did.' Kent's eyes were chips of honed steel, boring into the other. 'That is what I have to find out, who and why. Now, Nicholas, you were hanging round the market on the day Ned was killed in the stocks. Don't deny it. You were seen, and the constable has already questioned you.'

'I assure you, sir—'

'A man hangs for theft,' Kent scuffed some of the fallen coins with his foot, 'not only for murder.'

'There was a fight.' The words came out in a rush. 'It could have happened then.'

'It probably did, but I still have to discover *who* committed the crime. Kent stepped a pace closer. 'Think carefully, Nicholas, and tell me what you saw that day. You've already lied to me, you were thieving at the market. No,' he held up a hand, 'do not insult my intelligence by denying it. I could easily prove it, should I so desire. Let me put it to you that Ned, during his spell in the stocks, saw you. You knew that he saw, and there was just the chance that he *might* tip off Constable Symes, thereby lessening his own punishment for begging. You couldn't take that chance, so when the fight erupted you took advantage of the disturbance to silence him for good, maybe even using that handsome knife you were admiring upon my arrival. Or should I say gloating over. I think that you killed Ned the Beggar, Nicholas!'

'*It was the devil himself who killed old Ned!* ' Nicholas was whispering, glancing around the hovel as though he feared that Satan might be standing there. 'I know it was.'

'*How* do you know?'

'Because,' Nicholas's voice was a trembling whisper, the words were scarcely audible. '*Because. . . the night before, Ned fled, roaring his terror as if he had been branded with a red hot iron. And surely Lucifer was in pursuit. No mortal could create terror like that in any man!*'

'Tell me,' Kent rested a reassuring hand on the other's arm, 'and no harm will befall you. I will overlook your trickery and theft.'

'Ned was sleeping in the doorway of the charnel house.' Nicholas was tense, his eyes wide with fear. 'On a fine, warm night it was preferable to the stuffiness of the poor shelter. I saw him as I passed by, a bundle of rags hunched there. I, too, had decided to sleep out under the stars that night in a coppice on the edge of town. No sooner had I settled down than I heard what I thought was a frightened animal roaring. Then I saw Ned, running and shambling, screaming his terror. I crouched down for fear of what might be pursuing him. He passed within a few yards of me, headed into the forest. I did not see him again until next day when he was in the stocks. I thought perhaps he had been fleeing from the law — although nobody would be that frightened of the constable. Next I heard, he had been found stabbed.'

'Hmm.' Guy Kent stroked his chin thoughtfully. It was an elaborate tale, a lie that might well have matched the quick wit of Nicholas the coney-catcher, except that the fellow was too scared to have come up with it on the spur of the moment. It certainly had a ring of truth to it but, on the other hand, Nicholas was cunning, he had a glib tongue. 'Why didn't you tell this to the constable?'

'He would not have believed me.'

'And you think that I will?'

'I only tell you the truth, may God preserve me from Satan! Surely, it was the devil who pursued Ned, for Satan is amongst us or else the Witchfinder would not be here.'

'Somebody robbed the church, too.' Burglary and desecration were not crimes in keeping with Nicholas's furtive lifestyle; he relied upon quickness of wit and sleight of hand for his living.

'It was the devil, everybody knows that, even the constable. Mayhap he chased Ned because the beggar set eyes upon his awfulness.'

'An intriguing thought. Most intriguing, Nicholas, although methinks Satan would have struck the old man down there and then.'

'Unless he had his reasons. A foretaste of hell in the stocks, and then Lucifer sent one of his disciples to kill him.'

'Doubtless, the murderer is a disciple of the devil,' Kent was thoughtful, 'that much is certain, but I have my doubts that Ned was killed for the reason you put forward. Nevertheless, our talk has not been wasted. So Ned ran off into the woods. A flight of fear, undoubtedly, but where do you think he went from there? Did he hide out for the night and then return to town only to be arrested by the constable for begging? Or did he shelter elsewhere? I should be interested to hear your theory, Nicholas.'

'Only a fool would risk the woods after dark, for William, the gamekeeper, oft times sets mantraps. I think that Ned fled to the gypsy encampment, possibly was given shelter there until daylight. But I only surmise.'

'An intelligent supposition, too.' Kent turned towards the doorway. 'Romanies are known to offer help to those in trouble, it is part of their ancient code.'

'They will tell you nothing.' The colour had returned to Nicholas's cheeks. His relief was evident now that he had unburdened himself.

'Perhaps not, who knows? And take a tip from me, Nicholas, avoid the town for the moment. I hear that the Witchfinder is diligently searching out those who sup with the devil and he will not leave Stratford without torture and death.'

Guy Kent sauntered down to the river, seated himself on the bank and filled his clay pipe leisurely. There was no immediate urgency; he needed to think very carefully upon what the coney-catcher had told him before making his next move. Like the unwary wanderer in the forest at night, life was beset with many traps and pitfalls.

Satanic worship was providing false trails for his train of thought but he must not divorce himself entirely from it. For the dark deeds about him were undoubtedly, directly or indirectly, the work of the devil.

CHAPTER SIX

'He died of typhus fever, Kent!' The churchwarden's tone was an exaggerated warning. 'They're digging the grave right now; he'll be buried within the hour. A vagrant, of course. The poor shelter is alive with lice. See, even now, they're leaving his corpse in their dozens, just as if they've heard me and they don't want to be buried with him. But, by all means, go inside, look round all you want.'

Kent's mouth was dry; the stench wafting out from the charnel house was nauseating. Just one body, dressed in ragged garments, was stretched out on the stone floor. The gravediggers were working at full stretch to keep pace with the death toll: a heatwave was as bad as severe winter weather. Epidemics almost always spread out from the poor shelters, which was an underlying reason behind the new laws; rid the country of vagrants and reduce disease.

Guy Kent found the other's presence irritating. Wylde resented Kent's arrival in town in an official capacity, and he was combating it with an attitude of over-helpfulness.

'Is there anywhere or anything else you would like me to show you? I am at your service.'

'There's a few more people I have to talk to, churchwarden,' Kent said deliberately, disguising the irritation he felt, 'but now I'm just having a look round.'

'Have you the powers to arrest Satan?' Wylde was mocking him now.

'I certainly have the authority,' Kent smiled good-naturedly, 'but whether I can effect it is another matter.'

'Satan robbed the church, Kent, nothing is more certain. The Witchfinder identified certain marks on the altar steps – *cloven hoofprints!* He came himself, desecrated and stole. The parson is still poorly in bed, the physician visits him three times daily and has advised a bed-sitter for the night hours. On the Witchfinder's advice, garlic has been hung in the room. Not content with sacrilege and theft, Lucifer has smitten down one of God's servants. The Reverend Long may well die if his condition does not improve soon.'

'Perhaps Miss Hawker should take a look at him, churchwarden.'

'*No!* ' The refusal was spat out with venom. 'A godfearing man of the cloth like Long would not like to be administered to by a wen— a woman. One of self-confessed celibacy such as he might well suffer heart failure at the very mention of such a thing. Imagine, if she examined him, what parts of his anatomy hitherto unseen by female eyes throughout a life of self-imposed purity might be revealed to her gaze. Such a thought is unforgivable.'

'It was just an idea.' Kent experienced a feeling of smug satisfaction at having aroused the other's ire and hypocrisy. It was rumoured that Martyn Wylde was a womaniser but, if so, then the churchwarden kept his philanderings discreet. Public disapproval of Kent's cohabitation with Diana obviously still lingered within the close-knit circle of parochial administration. 'Anyway,' he shrugged his shoulders, 'I'm just going to have a look round on my own.'

'As you wish.' Wylde puffed his chest out in yet a further demonstration of his disapproval. 'Go where you will. None can stop you for you are commissioned by the Lord Lieutenant. But I fear you are wasting your time and the county's money. Ned was knifed in a fight at the Market Cross, and we shall never find the culprit. It might even have been an accident by a knife-wielding lout, for there is no obvious reason to murder a beggar. It would be far better if your mission was to track down those who stole from the church, although even that would be futile, for the Witchfinder is now convinced, beyond all doubt, that the act was carried out by the devil. He will arrest every witch in the town and its surrounding areas, a task which he has already embarked upon with some success. He needs no help. Indeed, an offer of assistance would be an insult to one whose reputation is respected throughout the land and who is answerable only to the Privy Council. Doubtless Jane, the whore, will confess and give the names of her fellow witches before the sun sets. Luke Jeffries is interrogating her even now in the cells beneath the town hall.'

Guy Kent's stomach balled, and he felt slightly sick. Sweat stung his eyes, distorted his vision.

'Are you all right? You don't look at all well, Kent.' The churchwarden's mocking voice seemed to come from far away. *I hope you're ill. I hope you die, then we'll be rid of your busybodying, taking up our valuable time when we're attempting to hunt down the witches who robbed and desecrated our church.*

'I'm all right.' The ground seemed to heave up, settled again. Kent wiped his eyes with the back of his hand. 'Just the heat.'

'You need to rest, Kent. May I presume and recommend the Swan Inn if you don't feel well enough to travel back to Newbold tonight.'

'Thank you, but I'll be fine.'

'Seek me out if you need me.' It was with some relief that Kent saw the other prepare to take his leave. 'And, if you take my advice, you'll stay clear of corpses that have died of typhus fever. The plague has similar symptoms. It's the lice that spread it, you know. Lice always desert a corpse when the flesh grows cold, and they look for another host then. I shall go and see what progress Luke Jeffries is making with his suspect. Good day to you.'

Kent leaned against the doorway of the charnel house, watched the churchwarden stride away down Chapel Street in the direction of the town hall. An imposing figure, there was no doubting the man's arrogance by his stride, the way he glanced contemptuously at a group of labourers drinking outside an ale house. The churchwarden demanded respect, seemed to savour the dislike of the townspeople. Wylde had only two months of office left and he was determined to make the most of them, to go down in history as the one who assisted the Witchfinder in his purge of those who communed with the devil.

Kent mopped his sweaty forehead with a green handkerchief. A glance inside this place of the dead showed him that the flies were swarming now. They seemed to sense that they had only a short time left in which to finish their repast before the body was taken from them. There was no sign of the lice. Kent wondered where they had gone, and shuddered. Beyond the church Kent heard the clink of shovels on stones; the gravediggers seemed to be working with a desperation in spite of the heat. Typhus was an ever-present threat.

He managed to convince himself there was nothing to be gained by entering the building. Ned had probably not gone inside until he was carried there and by then it was of no consequence. The beggar had spent the early part of his last night in this very porch where Guy Kent now stood, a pathetic figure huddled against the stonework. Within sight of the portals of the Holy Trinity church. The old man would not have been alerted by noise for he was deaf so he had to have seen whatever there was to see. This was where it had all begun, where Ned had embarked upon the last phase of his struggle for survival.

There was nobody in sight. Kent lowered himself down on to his haunches, wondered on which side of the doorway the old man had slept. A position from which he might have noticed the glow of a lantern. There was only one place, Kent peered closely at the rough stonework and that was when he spied a triangular shred of material adhering to it.

Carefully, for it shredded to his touch, he peeled it away. Frayed and rotting, it was undoubtedly raw hessian, the kind that the majority of vagrants wore, ill-fitting, worn-out winter labourers' garb, given to the destitute with mixed compassion rather than allowing it to smoulder in the hearth and fill the room with its pungent fumes. Sometimes throwout clothing was used to dress an effigy in garden or field in an attempt to scare away voracious birds which came in search of tender seedlings. Often beggars stole the scarecrows' clothes after dark.

Ned might well have acquired the garment from which this fragment had been ripped by such means. Or any of his colleagues who sheltered by night in the dilapidated establishment erected from parish funds for their meagre comfort.

Kent held the material close to his nose. His trained sense of smell detected the sour odour of a body that had never washed, filth

47

ingrained with the sweat of many summers.

Scores of bodies smelled like that. Presumption was a dangerous way in which to err; basic facts had to be established and often, even then, one ended up with a vague generalisation.

It was a long walk in the heat of the day out to that remote tumbledown barn which Nicholas was using for temporary shelter. Only his rigid discipline of attention to detail, however small, lent strength to Guy Kent's tired limbs. And when he arrived there, the building was empty; gone was the bedding, those trinkets and coins over which the coney-catcher had gloated.

A dead atmosphere, one which Kent sensed and recognised by experience: a kind of vacuum. The feeling of habitation was gone, blown away on the warm summer breeze that came up from the Avon.

There was no evidence of a hasty departure, nothing left behind in haste. The man had simply packed his belongings and left. Because he knew that Stratford was no longer a safe place. He would not be returning.

A cold shiver teased Kent's spine in spite of the oppressive heat. Nicholas had fled because he feared death in its various ways, the fevered suffering of typhus or the short sharp pain when the noose tightened and dislocated the neck. There was no way back from those, either.

The other might have lied, sent Kent on a fool's errand to give himself time to leave. The fabrication of a furtive mind, a deaf-mute roaring his inarticulate terror into the night as he fled from a terrible fate. Kent's intuition told him that Nicholas had spoken the truth. But, right now, the Lord Lieutenant's investigator was a long way from corroborating it.

Edmund was not at home in his cave on Guy's Cliff, either, but his absence was only temporary for a well-read bible and book of prayer were placed reverently upon a makeshift altar constructed of stone which had been carried, at no small expenditure of physical effort, from the nearby quarry.

Kent sat in the cave entrance and waited awhile, meditated upon a number of matters which were not all related to murder and witchcraft. A landscape that was steeped in legend still seven centuries after another Guy had lived in this place, looked upon this same river with its mallard fledgelings flapping across the surface as they strove to learn to fly; wild bees hunting pollen, the strain of crickets sawing away in the seeding grass. Of mythical dragons and a Dun Cow, and a great invading army from Denmark destroying everything in its path. Days of chivalry when knights wore shining armour and jousted for their honour.

He was proud to have been named after that ancient Guy. His mother had claimed that he was of the same bloodline; he chose to believe her, and that was enough for him, he wished neither to attempt to prove nor to disprove her belief.

Now there was another Dun Cow to be hunted down and slain. It would be no easier than in his ancestor's day. A challenge that fired him, had him rising to his feet, wending his way back down the narrow steep track.

In his mind he heard the cries of a damsel in distress. This time she was no lady of noble strain, rather a bedraggled whore screaming at the Witchfinder's repertoire of tortures as he strove to extract a confession from her.

Guy Kent increased his pace. He knew that when the sun had dipped behind the Welcombe Hills it would be too late. Time was running out for Jane. And for himself.

CHAPTER SEVEN

The end cell in the row of four was only used on those occasions when drunken disorder was rife in the town. Its heavy oaken and studded door had no grille, and inside this airless place the walls glistened with condensation and moss grew upon the rough stonework.

Whenever it was used for overnight incarceration, those prisoners who emerged the following morning with terror stamped on their faces attempted to convince themselves that what they had seen in there was nothing more than the figment of a drunken brain. For, to be sure, the Lord Lieutenant would not permit such a place to exist within a township which was fast earning respect throughout the country thanks to the works of the bard.

Adjustable chains with steel wristlets hung from iron rings in the far wall. A human body of any height could be suspended so that its feet dangled above the floor. On an adjacent table an assortment of whips were displayed, some with studded lashes; a pair of callipers that could grip and extract fingernails that had been deliberately cut short in an attempt to thwart it. A thumbscrew that was operated with a minimum of effort to effect maximum of pain. Tinder boxes and tapers to singe living flesh or burn off body hair. And a number of other devices which were referred to in hushed and frightened voices.

For this cramped dungeon of pain and slow death was reserved by the Crown for the visits of the Witchfinder. It was but a short wagon journey from here to the charnel house.

'Mr Jeffries is busy at present,' a stoic deputy constable on duty at the top of the flight of stone steps leading down below informed Guy Kent brusquely.

This time the long drawn out scream of pain was not in Kent's mind. It jarred every nerve in his body, cramped his stomach.

'By order of the Lord Lieutenant of Warwickshire.' He hastily unfolded a sheet of creased parchment, thrust it in front of the man's face. 'Lead the way, officer. I have no time to waste.'

Because, somewhere down there, a woman had already begun to die.

The other was clearly perplexed. His literacy was restricted to the recognition of the finely penned signature and waxed impression of a coat of arms which he had seen on other documents of importance. He dared not risk disobedience even though the Witchfinder's warrant bore the signature and seal of an even higher authority.

Uncertainly, clumsily, he descended the flight of steps. His duty was to carry out orders, it ended there. If there was to be conflict then it would be settled between Luke Jeffries and the man in green. He had no interest whatsoever in the eventual outcome so long as he was not charged with negligence.

Jane, the whore, was barely recognisable, her bruised naked body a mass of lash weals as it hung on the wall at full arms' length. Shapely, it might even have aroused Kent's desires in different circumstances and other surroundings. Here, it repulsed and angered him but, outwardly, he gave no sign of his feelings.

Luke Jeffries turned sharply as the door opened, his thin features depicting irritation at the sight of a stranger accompanying the guardian of the cells. His searching eyes looked for the churchwarden, the only person permitted to interrupt him, and then only with good reason.

50

'What is this, constable?' he asked in a deep voice, waved a deprecating hand. 'Can you not see that I am busy?'

'An envoy of the Lord Lieutenant, sir,' a faltering introduction, a half-wince as though he expected an instant reprimand.

Jeffries scanned the sheet of parchment, sucked his thin lips in perplexity. A tall dark man, in some ways he reminded Kent of Richard ap Cynon, almost swashbuckling except that cruelty exuded from his every expression and movement. He glanced at the prisoner; his sadistic pleasures were being disturbed and his vocation demanded dedication. Sunken cheeks, a decisiveness about his posture that came from years of having his actions go unquestioned. In spite of the heat – even down here the atmosphere was sticky and sultry – he wore his familiar long black coat and open breeches with fedora to match. Not so much as a droplet of sweat glistened on his high forehead in the light from the lantern above.

'What is your reason for disturbing me?' Gimlet eyes blazed a threat of retribution.

'A request to question the prisoner.' Kent forced himself to speak with respect. Nothing would be achieved by making demands of this man.

'I am interrogating her.'

'So I perceive, but I am conducting a separate enquiry, one that has no bearing on witchcraft.'

'And the crime?'

'Murder.'

Luke Jeffries's eyes flickered. 'Witches are murderers,' he hissed venomously.

'Not Jane. My own investigations have shown her to be innocent, but I believe her to have some information which might assist me in finding the murderer I seek.'

'She will confess, I promise you that.'

'Perhaps. Under torture. But I beg of you to let me speak with her first. Perhaps she will be able to help us both. Let me talk to her now before her brain becomes crazed with pain and she utters only illogical ramblings.'

'I see.' the Witchfinder turned, watched his prisoner, looking for a movement, the spasm of a pain-racked nerve or the flicker of an eyelid. There was neither. She hung limply, her head lolling forward. 'I think she is unconscious, but I have the means to revive her.' He chuckled softly, reached something from off the table behind him, lifted it up for Kent to see.

Kent's stomach churned again. The object in question was a tapered cylinder, cast in iron, some eight inches in length with a circumference of four inches at its base. Short spikes protruded from the sides, and at the thicker end there was a ring, wide enough for a finger to be inserted.

Jeffries smiled humourlessly, sadistically, as he demonstrated how it was possible to revolve the instrument with a forefinger, taking care to keep his free hand away from the revolving spikes.

'My own modification. Alas, I cannot claim to have invented it, although surely I would have done so had I been born a few years earlier. However, *I* named it. *The Iron Maiden.*'

'I see.'

'It has never yet failed to extract a confession.' A statement that was not intended as a boast. 'This woman's stubbornness has decreed that it must be used.'

'Wait! *Please.*' One never issued an order to the Witchfinder unless one sat on the Privy Council.

Jeffries glanced up. He was not accustomed to having his actions questioned. 'On whose command, whose humble request? I serve the highest authority in the land.'

'That I accept, and request.' Kent forced humility. It was not easy. 'As I said, she may well tell me things of her own volition.'

'She will tell me, have no doubts about that. She will scream her confession until these walls tremble, give me the names of her fellow witches, those who perpetrated this terrible act of desecration and the theft of God's possessions, that I assure you, Kent.' He rotated the instrument of torture again; it made a grinding and clanking sound. 'I will ask her your questions, too, if you tell me what it is that you wish to know.'

'Witchfinder.' Kent was pleading now; humility was all that was left if Jane was to be spared the agony and degradation of this vile method of torture. 'Would you, in your generosity, grant me a few minutes alone with this woman? It can surely make no difference to your ultimate plans for her.'

'Alone?' Dark eyebrows rose, those bloodless lips were drawn back in a snarl which embodied suspicion. 'Why *alone*? Will there be questions and answers which are not for my ears? Is this some cunning subterfuge?'

'I assure you, it is nothing of the kind.'

'Perhaps, then, you seek the pleasures of her helpless body?' The other's face was thrust close to Kent's, the snarl became a leer. 'Her

52

final enjoyment of physical pleasure before the Iron Maiden destroys it for ever, eh?'

'No, no, nothing of the kind.' Kent was sickened by the suggestion, despised the Witchfinder for even presuming it. 'Delicate matters concerning a murder. I hope to extract names from her which might create a scandal in the parish. *If* she has the information I require, I think she will only divulge it to me. You understand, Witchfinder. . .'

'Ah!' A change of tone, an attitude that bordered on complicity. 'In that case, I see no reason why not.'

'Thank you, Witchfinder, you are most kind.'

'But only for a short while.' The tall man nodded in the direction of the waiting officer. 'I am in need of some light refreshment. I shall return shortly, and then you must leave immediately. I cannot allow an extension of my gracious generosity towards even an ambassador of the Lord Lieutenant himself.'

'I shall leave when requested.' Kent bowed, hated himself for it.

'The officer will remain on guard at the top of the steps.' *Just in case you have any ulterior motive.* 'I shall return within the half-hour.'

It was with no small amount of relief that Kent heard the key turning in the lock, footsteps receding down the passageway.

'Jane?'

Her eyes opened, her swollen and bruised lips attempted a smile. A whisper that was scarcely audible, so that he had to lean forward. 'They'll kill me, Guy, whatever you try to do. You are only prolonging my agony.'

'There's a chance.' He found the pulley, lowered her a few inches so that her feet rested on the floor, brought a gasp of relief from her. 'You're no witch, Jane.'

'No, but there are rumours. They have to persecute somebody. The Witchfinder needs a scapegoat.'

'All the same, somebody robbed and desecrated Holy Trinity, we can't deny that.'

'I have no idea who it was, I swear.'

'I believe you.' He rummaged in his belt pouch, produced the strip of hessian. 'Do you recognise this? It came from somebody's clothing, a person who slept in the doorway of the charnel house.'

'I know it,' her eyes narrowed, 'by the weave. Coarse, rather than the fine texture of labouring cloth. The garment was fashioned from corn sacks. It belonged to Ned the Beggar, I'm certain.'

He felt a surge of satisfaction at confirmation of his hunch. 'Yes, I thought it did. Jane, Ned passed part of that fateful night in the doorway of the charnel house, as we both know. I believe that something frightened him, terrified him so that he fled in fear of his life. Maybe he saw the robbers. . . or something worse! He ran to the woods. Nicholas, the coney-catcher, saw him. Have you any idea where he was between the time he fled and when he was arrested at daylight in the town?'

'He went to the gypsy encampment.'

'How do you know?'

She hesitated, closed her eyes at the pain in her tortured body. 'Cornelius told me. I was on my way back from the camp when the constables arrested me.'

He did not ask her reason for visiting the Romanies. Time was short, and it was probably irrelevant anyway. 'Jane, there's just a chance that might save you.'

'That is most unlikely. Jeffries is savouring every moment of my torture. He would not miss it for a ransom.'

'Unlikely or not, we have to try anything. The Witchfinder is open to a deal. The catching of the robbers, whether Satanists or just thieves, will enhance his reputation with the Privy Council and that is the most important thing in life to him. We know that Ned slept within sight of the church, saw something, fled for his life. Now, just suppose that Ned was in league with the robbers, tipped them off, acted as a lookout.'

'That's impossible!' She almost laughed. 'He would have neither the wit nor the strength.'

'I agree, but it is a possibility. Then Ned was knifed in the stocks to ensure his silence.' Kent stiffened. In the recesses of this dungeon jail his keen hearing detected heavy footfalls that could only be the deputy constable returning.

'Remember one thing, Guy,' she, too, had heard the approaching footsteps, 'the eyes of the deaf and dumb miss nothing! They are the keenest of all.'

'Here's what you must do. . .' He spoke with a whispered urgency, knew that he gambled with her life. A key grated in the door. 'Nobody, not even the Witchfinder, can harm the dead.'

'Well.' Luke Jeffries stood framed in the doorway, glowered his disapproval at the slackening of the arm chains. 'It would appear that this is nothing less than a time-wasting ploy to earn the witch a brief respite from her sufferings.'

'On the contrary,' Kent's eyes met the other's, 'our discussion has been most informative for all concerned.'

'And you have your confession?'

'I have the information I came here seeking, for all the good it will do me. Witchfinder, I have presumed to make a bargain on your behalf.'

Sallow cheeks tinged with pink, Jeffries drew himself up haughtily. 'On my behalf ? Sir, you have the cheek of the devils whom we propose to bring to the gallows!'

'It is to our mutual benefit.' Guy Kent was undeterred. 'This woman is innocent of witchcraft, I stake my life and my reputation on it. Her only sin is whoring and that is neither your concern nor mine. In return for naming those who perpetrated the crime in the church, I have promised her freedom. I trust you will agree, for we cannot always guarantee a confession under torture.'

'How dare you, sir!'

'Very well, I shall submit my report to the Lord Lieutenant who in turn will report to the bishop and the Privy Council. It will be up to them to decide, to consider the authenticity of conflicting stories. Meantime, the culprits go free. I will take my leave now and let you do as you see fit, Witchfinder!'

'Wait!' Jeffries barred the way, uncertainty in his expression.

'The decision is yours, Witchfinder.'

The other pondered, stroked his angular chin. 'How will I know that she is telling the truth?'

'Would you be any more certain with her writhing in agony, uttering a name, any name, to spare herself further torture?'

'And your murderer?'

'One and the same, it seems, as those who communed with the devil. Hear it from her own lips.'

'*Tell me!*' The Witchfinder whirled on Jane. '*Give me the names of those responsible and you shall have your freedom!*'

'Ned the Beggar plotted it with a gang of thieves.' She shied from his fearsome countenance. 'He was their lookout, but when their foul deed was done they sought to murder him to ensure his silence. He escaped but was arrested for begging and put in the stocks. Later that day they returned to town and stabbed him.'

'How do you know this?' There was suspicion in his narrowed eyes.

'The Romanies told me. Ned sought refuge there but they turned him away for fear that they might be implicated in the crime.'

'And *who* were the robbers?' His expression was one of mingled anger and triumph. 'Tell me this very minute!'

'The moonmen!'

'It fits perfectly.' Kent smacked a fist into the palm of his hand. 'This band of roaming thieves have been hanging round the surrounding villages for the past week. There have been reports of poultry thefts. Itinerants, a camouflage for witchcraft, they came here purposely to rob the church. Who better than a halfwit beggar for their stooge?'

'These men must be brought before the justices forthwith.' Jeffries whirled on the deputy constable. 'Send word to the churchwarden and the constable, have them saddle up a detachment of armed men and ride at once to apprehend the moonmen!'

'They left town the night after the robbery,' the man replied.

'To be sure they did! Ride them down, hunt them out wherever they are skulking, send a messenger to warn the Lord Lieutenants of all the adjoining counties for, I promise you, boundaries shall not offer them sanctuary!'

'And catch the murderers I am seeking, too,' Kent added piously, 'for it would seem that we were hunting one and the same, Witchfinder.'

'So it *seems*.' Jeffries cast a glance at Jane. 'Very well, you shall have your freedom for the time being. But, I warn you, should these men prove not to be the villains, then your suffering shall be tenfold. You will find nowhere to hide from me. And, Kent, I hope, for your sake, that you will not make a fool of me, for if that should be the case you also will pay dearly. The woman is free to go for the moment.'

Kent left town with mingled feelings: relief because Jane had been spared the sufferings of a witch, doubt over truths and half-truths. It was unlikely that the moonmen would be caught. If they were, then they would be executed for witchcraft and robbery instead of for poultry theft. The noose was impartial; the outcome was the same.

A fabrication that might have been the truth; guesswork was a dangerous game to play. Meantime, he had diverted the churchwarden and the Witchfinder, it gave him a breathing space. Ned had fled to the Romanies and they had turned him away. Whither had the beggar gone then? Was there some factor between his leaving the gypsy camp and being arrested by the constable that had brought about his death?

He needed to talk at length with Jane. Their brief discussion in the torture chamber had been aimed at saving her life. Did she know more about what had happened to Ned and for some reason chose not to tell?

Something she had said kept repeating itself in the recesses of his troubled mind as if it was attempting to give him guidance.

The eyes of the deaf and dumb are keenest of all.

CHAPTER EIGHT

Jane's tumbledown one-roomed cottage nestled just off the road to Banbury, screened from travellers by an overgrowth of hawthorn and elder, a wilderness that had its attraction in a mass of wild flowers that had gone unchecked and successfully resisted the attempts of couch grass to choke them.

The wooden gate had long rotted, just a broken off post remaining as a memento; beyond it a well-trodden path wove through a forest of blossoming elders. Only after the second bend, when one emerged into a patch of lupins and wild willow herb, was the dwelling visible. The thatched roof had blackened; there was a gaping hole where the rain lashed the unprotected rafters. The porch tilted, threatened to collapse beneath the weight of rambling wild rose creepers, and the warped door was ajar; it required no small amount of physical effort to force it shut.

Guy Kent left his mount tethered in the shade of a huge chestnut tree at the roadside. His mind was still uneasy, with a nagging premonition again that something was wrong. He consoled himself with the reminder that a lot was wrong in this town and its surrounding countryside, had been so since that fateful day last week when Ned was murdered in the stocks. The Witchfinder had ridden off with a band of armed constables on the trail of the moonmen. Martyn Wylde had been gone since yesterday, away to Warwick to submit his own report to the Lord Lieutenant. It was as though a temporary lull had settled over Stratford.

Kent hesitated at the remains of the gate. A fleeting sensation of guilt, mostly because Diana did not like him coming here; she knew his visit was on official business but there was disapproval, nay jealousy, in her expression as she had bidden him farewell. Men slunk to this very cottage for pleasures in addition to those enjoyed in the marital bed. Guy had saved Jane from torture and death; might she not in her gratitude seek to reward him in ways that had no bearing upon his investigations? A temptress in rags, a shapely body in spite of its weals and bruises and grimed dirt.

He shrugged off the feeling, stepped on to the pathway of flattened grasses, avoided a patch of nettles for they stung viciously even through well-woven nether socks.

A sense of apprehension had him holding back. He asked himself again whether it was really necessary for him to interrogate Jane; if the Witchfinder caught up with the moonmen there would be scapegoats aplenty, and the investigation would be closed. Ned had been knifed in the scuffle in the Market Cross. The details were irrelevant, nothing was to be gained by pursuing the matter further.

He moved forward. He did have to speak with Jane for his own peace of mind. He needed to know where Ned had spent the remainder of that awful night.

A jackdaw *cawed* from the thatch, it sounded like *go-back*. Kent paused in his step, eyed it defiantly. It was not afraid of Man, for this place was its domain, its sanctuary; it was merely lodging a corvine protest at the disturbance.

A mangy cat darted out of the partly open door, a black streak as it fled for the cover of the surrounding undergrowth. A rustle and then it was gone.

But he knew it was watching him, he felt its eyes upon him just like those of the jackdaw up on the rooftop. The bird opened its wings as if to fly away, changed its mind and closed them again. Still and silent, a vulture in the desert watching from afar, waiting for its victim to die before it flew in to scavenge.

Kent shivered. This was silly, he was letting his feelings get the better of him. Defiant, determined, he strode towards the doorway.

He stood on the threshold, for once uncertain of himself. Extended knuckles tapped the woodwork almost nervously. It would have been presumptuous to enter even a whore's abode uninvited. His knocking echoed inside the gloomy, near derelict, abode. It had an empty sound about it, a hollowness like the beating of an empty barrel.

He licked his dry lips. Jane could be resting, exhausted by her ordeal. Or she might have gone out, she was well known for her long walks in the wooded Welcombe Hills. She didn't *have* to be at home in the middle of a sweltering summer's day. He had no right to expect her to be.

He knocked again, more firmly this time. The echoes were thunderous; mentally he cringed from them. Behind him a clump of mugwort rustled. He whirled around. A feline head showed amidst the tall stems, watching him intently. *What business have you with my mistress? Are you not ashamed of what men have inflicted upon her already?*

Kent was sweating profusely; he almost apologised to the cat. Jane wasn't here, and he should not waste time hanging about on the off chance of her returning shortly. Or should he? Officially the case was solved, the villains were being chased, but, in the meantime, there were still too many unanswered questions about this whole business. He would not allow himself to pander to a guilty conscience because of Diana's disapproval. Far better to make sure that Jane wasn't here, or that she was just sleeping, than to leave with uncertainty.

The door was wedged firmly on the uneven soil floor. It was nigh impossible to force it wider; probably Jane just squeezed through the gap. He managed likewise with an effort, boyish as his figure was. Outside, the cat *miaowed* as if in protest at this unauthorised entry.

The room was stuffy, a bread oven that had not cooled down. Only a lone shaft of sunlight that slanted through the partly open door alleviated the darkness in the single, windowless chamber. He had to wait for his eyesight to adjust to the gloom.

A jumble of untidiness, rumpled empty bedding thrown back in the far corner, a rough wooden table piled with cooking utensils and unwashed clothes; cat scratchings in the soil by the well. A hearth full of dead ashes.

So empty. So *dead*.

'Jane?' His voice quavered, his call little louder than a whisper. It seemed to hang in the sultry atmosphere, mocking him.

Well, she wasn't in here, not that he had searched every nook and cranny of the interior. If she hid, fearing the return of the Witchfinder, then she would almost certainly recognise his voice even if she could not recognise him in the half-light.

'Jane, it's me. Guy Kent.' His voice sounded flat, and he swallowed as if he was embarrassed by his trespass. 'Are you—'

He sensed a movement, spun round and saw her. She was stark naked, her slim body still disfigured by the previous day's ordeal. Her swollen lips were wide as if she was about to call out a greeting; her eyes bulged in their sockets like air bubbles about to burst.

Then he saw that her feet did not touch the floor, dangled a few inches above it. Her body moved again, swung to face him, and it was then that he noticed the rope cutting deep into her slender neck, and his eyes followed it upwards to where the woven hemp was knotted around a rusted meat hook in the overhead beam.

Jane's reprieve from execution had been short-lived. Here, in her own abode, she hung by the neck and she was very dead.

Kent stared, hoped that it was some kind of hallucination, maybe the heat or a trick of the half-light, that Jane was just standing there, her expression a result of her inquisition by the Witchfinder.

'Jane!' This time he yelled her name, in the vain hope that it would jerk her back into life. But he had seen too many corpses in his time not to recognise this one for what it was.

It took him a few seconds to get himself back under control. His first reaction was one of anger; towards the Witchfinder who had perpetrated such atrocities upon a fellow being; towards the law which not only permitted such inhumanity but actually encouraged it. Jane was no witch, only malicious gossip amongst the womenfolk who feared for their husbands' fidelity had branded her one, as surely as the lashes of Luke Jeffries's assortment of whips had left their weals upon her.

Then he saw the log, a chunk of tree stump cut by the foresters and somehow transported back here by Jane, probably to use as a pillow. It had toppled from beneath her dangling feet. Or else she had kicked it away when. . .

Her arms hung limply by her sides. In the case of a murderous hanging her wrists would have been lashed behind her back. A flashback in his mind; Jane, humiliated and deranged by physical pain, had seen in her anguish a way in which to thwart her tormentors, for doubtless the Witchfinder would return for her in due course. *Thou shalt not execute me. I will hang myself, taunt you with the sight of my swinging body, deprive you of the pleasure of seeing me kick my last. None shall see me; when they find me it will all be over. Do as thou wilt with my corpse, for I am beyond your reach now.*

A groan of sorrow escaped Guy Kent's lips. He stretched out a hand and clasped Jane's cold fingers, squeezed them. 'Oh, my poor, poor girl, if only you had waited for me. It need not have ended this way.'

From the doorway the cat yowled its own sympathy and from up above the jackdaw called mournfully. As if Jane had had an affinity with them, as doubtless the locals would have confirmed.

'If only you could speak and tell me how it happened,' Kent said to the animal. It turned and fled.

Slowly, gently, he cut the taut rope with his knife, reverently lowered Jane to the ground. Her lips seemed as if they were straining to speak, her dead eyes met his own as if they saw.

It was then that his foot kicked against something; a small object that clinked metallically as it struck a stone. The beam of sunlight fell upon it and it scintillated.

Kent stooped and picked it up, trailed a length of broken chain with it. A crucifix, it nestled in the palm of his hand. There was a letter of the alphabet engraved upon its base. 'E'.

Kent's lips tightened. He felt his anger returning until he shook with silent rage.

'Oh, you, a man of God, to have stooped so low. I would never have believed it in a hundred years!'

He went outside, untethered his horse, and rode it until its flanks were flecked with sweat. Only when he came within sight of that wooded cliff did he slow his pace.

And *here* of all places, the shrine of his own valiant ancestor who had fought nobly in the crusades. It was as much a sacrilege as the desecration of the church to the man in green.

It made Guy Kent very angry.

This time Edmund, the homeless monk, was in his temporary sanctuary.

He was deep in prayer before his makeshift altar, his tonsured head bowed over his book of prayer, when Kent burst into the cave.

'Man, we have some talking to do!' Kent grabbed the other by his habit, dragged him up to his feet.

Edmund's pink complexion paled and he gave a shrill, frightened squeak. The prayer book fluttered to the ground like a swatted moth.

Kent tore at the neck of the woollen garment, pulled it open to bare the naked flesh, saw the grimed mark left by a necklace that was no longer there. His lips were a tight bloodless line, his eyes burned with an anger which he could not guarantee to control.

'You dropped this!' He held the small bronze crucifix close to the other's rotund face, saw Edmund go cross-eyed, staring at it in amazement.

'Yes, it's mine. . . I had no idea I had dropped it, I never even missed it. Thank you, my friend. It means much to me, not just as a symbol of God but because it was given to me by Friar Egbert at the monastery where I spent my youth. He was a father to me, he—'

'You dropped it by Jane's body!' Kent spoke tersely, accusingly, did not relax his grip on the other.

'Yes, yes, I must have, I was so upset. Had I had a knife, I would have cut her down, laid her at peace. I am praying for her soul even now. Perhaps you would care to join me.'

'You'll rot in hell for what you did!' Edmund's teeth rattled as Kent shook him. 'You even tried to make it look like suicide. You might have fooled even me except that you left your cross behind. Man of God, pah! You're a man of the devil, and you're going to tell me what I want to know before we leave here, monk!'

'Sir, there must be some mistake!' Edmund was deathly white now. 'I found the poor soul hanging in her dwelling. I looked inside because there was no answer to my knockings. *She was already dead when I arrived, may God help me!* I will swear it on the bible, on my oath. I did not kill her!'

It was more than a panic protest. Kent had listened to false and genuine pleas of innocence many times before. In his own mind he had learned to detect the difference between lies and the truth. Edmund's eyes were wide, meeting his own; the other was frightened but he did not have an expression of guilt. Guy's hunches were not always infallible but he had a certain amount of faith in them.

'All right.' Slowly Kent released his grip, stood back and folded his arms. 'You arrived at Jane's cottage, she was already hanging from the beam. But did you go to call upon her? Or is that an indiscreet question? Tell me the truth else you'll be tried for murder!'

'No, no!' Indignation at the suggestion. 'I am celibate, sir, I have never lain with a woman, nor will I. I heard how she had been tortured by the Witchfinder; I went to comfort one who had been unjustly accused and had suffered in her innocence. That was my only reason for calling on her.' He reached behind him for the bible on the altar. 'I will swear it before God and yourself, sir.'

'Later, perhaps.' Kent waved away the bible. 'But I want to ask you another question, Edmund. On the night the Holy Trinity church was desecrated, did you by any chance glimpse Ned the Beggar, wherever you might have been yourself?'

'I did not, but I know that he went to the gypsies in the wood, seeking sanctuary.'

'And how do you know that?'

'Because I, too, asked them for refuge. Some of them were preparing to leave, go elsewhere, and I thought that perhaps I might ride with them. Tramping the roads, day after day, seeking shelter by night, is irksome after a number of years. I thought that perhaps I might join up with them for a while, travel with them, spread the word of God, and perhaps even convert them from their pagan beliefs.'

'You will not manage that, methinks.' Kent smiled at the thought. 'Romanies have their own beliefs; nothing will change them. So Ned fled to them but they turned him away. Have you any idea where he went from there?'

'No, I did not ask. It was of no consequence to myself.'

'I see. So you were abroad in the forest that night, running the gauntlet of William the gamekeeper's mantraps. Did you meet with any others?'

'Sir, you mistake me, it was only yesterday that I requested shelter from the gypsies. They told me about Ned then. But I was sleeping out on the edge of the woods that night. I feared to enter because of the devilish traps you mention. Yes, I saw others, those whom people refer to as the "moonmen", a furtive and untrustworthy band of men if ever there was one.'

'Going to the woods?'

'Aye, and carrying heavy sacks, but I have no idea of the contents.'

'It could have been stolen poultry; geese, maybe.' Kent looked thoughtful.

'And I will tell you something else, sir.'

'Yes?'

'After his absence from the district, Nicholas is back.'

'The coney-catcher! In Stratford town or the forest?'

'Neither. I glimpsed him in the turnip field alongside Jane's cottage. I had forgotten it until now. He hid when he heard me coming, I think perhaps he had heard of the poor lady's misfortunes and was planning to steal from her house. Not that she had anything worth stealing. Or perhaps, thinking her still to be in jail, he planned to live there. I just thought that I would mention it.'

'Most interesting, monk.' Kent suddenly stiffened. His keen hearing had detected sounds outside the cave, the tread of heavy boots ascending the steep slope, the muttered cursings of men sweltering in the heat of the day. 'Edmund, we have company, I think.'

Shadows fell across the entrance to the cave, and then the silhouettes of men were framed against the bright sunlight outside. Kent recognised the tall outline of the Witchfinder, stooping to peer inside. Behind him were a medley of pistol-carrying constables.

'The villain is here, men. Bring him out. Shoot if he resists, but only to wound. I want him to stand trial.' Jeffries stiffened in surprise, shaded his eyes in order to see into the cavern. 'Do my eyes play mischievous tricks upon me, or do I perceive the Lord Lieutenant's jack-in-office here also?'

'It is me,' Kent turned to face the newcomers, 'but I wonder if your reasons for coming here to arrest the monk are different from mine, Witchfinder?'

'He is the one whom we have been hunting the parish for!' A bony forefinger was stabbed accusingly at Edmund. 'Your story about the robbers had only a slight truth in it, Kent. Maybe, or maybe not, the beggar kept watch for them, that is irrelevant. Suffice it was the moonmen who looted the church, but he who hatched the plot stands before us now, the devil's disciple cloaked as a man of God to fool us. Maybe Jane, the witch, corrupted him with her spells – that we shall discover in due course. The constables will arrest her once we have this servant of Lucifer in jail. First, though, we must search the cave and its surrounds, for the stolen artefacts are hidden here somewhere!'

'And how do you know all this?' Kent's voice, his posture, verged on arrogance. His brain swirled with new confusion.

'The moonmen have confessed to the robbery and desecration. Quite readily, in fact; it took but the extraction of one toenail for their leader to scream out the guilt of them all. A messenger was sent on ahead to inform the churchwarden and request him to arrange a trial for tomorrow. These men will, doubtless, be publicly hanged, but it remains to be seen what form of execution will be deemed suitable for one who has sought to overthrow the Church with witchcraft. Hanging is for common thieves, witches are usually burned. Perhaps death by *pressing* will be deemed more suitable for one of such evil villainy!'

Kent felt physically sick; bile scorched his throat. Only once before had he known a 'pressing'. *Peine forte et dure*, the slow death, was sometimes the sentence passed on those who refused to plead or remained mute. The law stated that the prisoner should be laid naked on a floor and stones and iron placed upon him to the greatest bearable weight; on the following day he should be given three morsels of bread and no water; on the second day he should be given water but no bread; and this should be his diet until he died.

'I believe the monk is innocent,' Kent said.

'His trial will determine that.' The Witchfinder's voice was heavy with undisguised elation. 'I think, sir, that this is one case for which you will not be able to claim the credit. We shall see.' He turned to the constables behind him. 'Men, search this cave, look for loose rocks and a hole in the floor in which the stolen goods might be buried. Two of you take this devil in monk's habit to the chamber to await my return.'

Kent sat his horse, watched as Edmund, his hands bound behind his back, a rope tied round his waist, was forced to stumble in their wake. Once he fell, was dragged mercilessly for several yards before they allowed him to rise.

In the cave behind, Kent heard the clang of shovels on stone, the cursings of Luke Jeffries as he exhorted his men to greater efforts.

Kent shook his head in bewilderment. The moonmen had confessed under torture, that was no proof of their guilt; the Witchfinder needed scapegoats. Jane had been found hanged. Edmund's story had a ring of truth to it but, undoubtedly, the homeless monk would be executed. Who had killed Jane the whore? Could it be the murderer of Ned the Beggar, another seemingly motiveless killing? And why had Nicholas, the coney-catcher, been watching Jane's cottage? All questions that had to be answered.

And as he urged his horse slowly back in the direction of Newbold-on-Stour, it seemed as though he heard Jane's voice, shrill and urgent, coming from beyond the grave.

The eyes of the deaf and dumb are keenest of all.

What and whom had Ned seen on that fateful night, and where had he fled after the Romanies had refused him shelter?

CHAPTER NINE

The prospect of a witch trial created a fever of excitement in Stratford from the moment the moonmen and Edmund were brought into town. Relief, too, because the Witchfinder had caught his men and would be moving on elsewhere within a day or two.

By early evening the gallows was being erected on a patch of waste ground adjacent to Henley Street; it was presumed that the robbers would be hanged. Their principal crime was robbery, they had merely been used by the monk who was doubtless a disciple of the devil.

His fate was a matter of speculation; generally burning alive was the punishment especially inflicted on witches. It was decreed that no witch should be allowed to live, and thousands of wretched men and women, by their own confession, had suffered this fate over the centuries. Some five hundred a year were executed in this manner, and Luke Jeffries was proud of his own record of a thousand in his period of office.

Ducking and drowning were also a possibility, as was hanging, but as the church had been violated then surely some spectacular means of death would be decreed. Wagers were rife on the mode of death for Edmund; the favourite was burning. A stake was driven into the ground a short distance from the line of gallows, dry kindling from the woods heaped around it. Should the justices of the peace decide upon some other form of execution, then a celebration bonfire would be lighted at dusk.

The morrow would be a day of celebration akin to a fair; ale and cider would flow freely, the revelling would last the night through.

Only one form of execution would disappoint the expectant crowds: *peine forte et dure*, for that torturous death would be inflicted upon the victim in the confines of the dreaded cell set aside for the visits of Luke Jeffries. No spectators would be allowed. Nevertheless, a crowd would gather outside the town hall to await the announcement of the victim's death. Wagers would be laid on the time it would take; it was a lengthy process and might last several days, depending upon the resilience of the condemned. And Edmund the Monk was generally reputed to be hale and hearty.

Perhaps the monk might be hanged, drawn and quartered, it was whispered in the ale houses, for in some instances Queen Elizabeth had ordered such punishment for recusant priests and did not Edmund's crime warrant such a spectacular end? It was no small wonder that, considering the vileness of his crime, he had not been transported to the capital to suffer his fate so that it might be a lesson to witches throughout the land. That would, indeed, have been a disappointment for the townspeople of Stratford.

The night was a long one. It seemed that none slept, for there was constant activity in the streets. The robbers' trial would undoubtedly be a swift one for they had already confessed; they would be sentenced and taken straightway from the court for execution. A hundred or so people had elected to sleep on the ground by the gallows; the crowd would swell after daylight and those not gifted with height might be deprived of a view. Regrettably, hanging was swift, over all too quickly. But, hopefully, that would only be the start of events. A burning lasted much longer.

Kent rode into Stratford in the half-darkness prior to dawn, hunched in the saddle, for he had not slept. There were too many questions still unanswered. Already he doubted the guilt of those arrested. Even if Edmund had hanged Jane, Kent doubted the monk's involvement in the robbery of the church. But, there again, hunches were not always to be relied upon.

Six horsemen reined in their mounts in front of the town hall. By the glow of the lights from that building Guy Kent recognised every one of them; Talbot Christie, Edgar Ridge, Robert Dudley; Victor Gask was the first to tether his horse, William Hodge and Samuel Train dismounted stiffly for it had been a long ride and they were getting on in years. The Jury of Tenants. Only six had been summoned for service today, other times it might have been twenty. Because the defendant had already been judged guilty, a jury was a mere formality. The object was to execute a witch at all cost; the moonmen were incidental.

Kent sat his horse across the street, watched with tired but still keen eyes. The Witchfinder was doubtless down in his torture chamber. He had probably worked throughout the night, not just on a confession but in an attempt to discover the hiding place of the stolen artefacts.

Kent doubted whether Edmund would be able to reveal it.

Sunrise. It seemed that the world and his wife had come to town. Martyn Wylde had to shout for a path to be cleared for his horse; the street was packed from side to side. Only the presence of the Witchfinder gave the churchwarden authority to pass sentence. Had it been a straightforward murder trial then the Lord Lieutenant would have appointed a judge. Today he had sent Roland Packard, his chief justice of the peace, a small man with a wisping grey beard who constantly brushed dust from his fine velvet jacket.

Kent took his horse to the stables, paid the ostler. The man winked, gave a coarse whisper. 'There's goin' to be sommat worth seein' in a bit, sir, you mark my words. Rumour 'as it that they're goin' to hang the monk, then draw and quarter 'im. I seed it done once. back in eighty-three. . .'

'Rumours are generally unfounded and predictions invariably

wrong.' The man in green turned, walked from the building.

'*Hang the robbers. Burn the witch!*' The cry was taken up right the way down Chapel Street.

Edmund, the homeless monk, did not stand a chance. The judiciary would bow to public opinion today; it served to keep the loyalty of the rabble.

Kent fought his way through the crowd until he reached the steps of the town hall. He showed his authority to the constable on duty, filed through to the seats reserved for those privileged to watch a trial. He thought he heard muffled screams coming from below, winced and tried to close his ears to the sound.

That was when Jane spoke to him again. *The eyes of the deaf and dumb are keenest of all.*

Heavy-booted footfalls sounded in the passageway that led up from the cells. The moonmen had been brought to meet their inevitable fate.

The trial of the four nomadic poultry thieves took less than a quarter of an hour. Bowed and silent, they stood whilst the charges against them were read; that they did commune with the devil through his disciple and, as a result, set forth to commit an act of desecration and sacrilege under his spell; that a beggar, since deceased, was set to watch and to warn them of the approach of anyone who might raise the alarm. Then, having damaged and defaced, they stole, and in the woods they did give their ill-gotten gains to one Edmund, who had disguised himself as a monk. Then they fled, planning to return at a later date to collect a reward for their vile deeds, but were duly apprehended and imprisoned, where they confessed readily to their criminous acts. How did they plead?

Inarticulate grunts were taken as an admission of guilt in unison.

Roland Packard looked up. His eyes swept the seated Jury of Tenants. A unanimous acknowledgement was all that he needed. He stared glazedly at the guilty, for he had had no opportunity to sleep off his previous nights drinking.

A tap of his gavel. 'Sentenced to hanging.' His voice was barely audible. Another tap of his gavel and the constables moved forward to grab the only four men in the room who seemed unaware of what was happening.

A cheer went up from the waiting crowd as the wagon bearing the moonmen hove into view. People pushed and scrambled out of the way to afford it a passage. The constables were in a hurry, eager to return to the court to listen to the trial of the monk.

The Reverend Samuel Long would probably have been in attendance had his condition not worsened these last few days. It was feared by his physician that he would die before the end of the week. But godless men needed no preacher in their final hour.

They took the big red-bearded one first, had some difficulty in getting him up the short flight of wooden steps, not because he resisted but on account of his size and the way his legs refused to function. From a distance it seemed that his left leg might be broken; in court he had stood on his right and leaned on one of his companions.

'Hang the robbers!'

There was no ceremony; the noose was slipped around his neck, pulled tight. The crowd pushed forward. A woman screamed that she was being crushed but none heeded her. Others stretched up to their full height so that they might be afforded a clearer view.

It was over in the winking of an eye. the moonman's weight was instrumental in breaking his neck instantly. There was a delay as his executioners struggled to free his corpse, dragged it to one side. The second man was already being pulled up the steps.

This one was lighter. His frailty prolonged his agony, a choking and kicking figure who finally drowned in his own vomit.

The third victim's neck was skinned and stretched, until his death throes resembled those of an ostrich. The fourth had an uncanny resistance to death; the constables crowded round his twitching body, and the dull thuds which reached the strained ears of the watchers indicated that he had been despatched by clubbing.

The crowd whistled and jeered; a pleasure that should have been prolonged and savoured had, instead, been hastily and clumsily brought to a conclusion.

They watched the bodies being loaded on to the charnel cart, did not even notice the swarming flies.

'Bring out the witch. *Burn the witch!'*

Kent was visibly shocked and sickened at the sight of Edmund's condition as the monk was roughly assisted into court. Deathly white, in stark contrast to his ripped habit, his toes still seeped blood where every nail had been cruelly extracted. His hands were clenched so that it was impossible to see whether he still retained his fingernails. In all probability, he did not.

His eyebrows were gone, his forehead scorched and blistered from the flame of the taper. His garment was torn where his torturer had ripped the material to reach those parts upon which he wished to inflict pain rather than unclothe his unfortunate victim.

A man in a trance, numbed with agony, rendered dumb by shock. A stool was brought for him to sit upon for there was no way he would have been able to stand unassisted.

The charge: that you did cohort with Lucifer, your master, in an endeavour to destroy and rob the house of God. That, together with your accomplices, you did bury the stolen articles in a place so far undiscovered, and that to avoid arrest you did murder one beggar and one whore. How do you plead?

Edmund's animal-like grunt was neither a denial nor an admission of his guilt. His bloodied tonsured head hung low and did not move. He might not even have heard; or if he had, he did not understand.

Packard glanced at the churchwarden as though seeking guidance, cleared his throat. The silence in the court was pregnant. At the back of the room, his dark clothes blending with the shadows, sat the Witchfinder, head bowed as if he was deep in thought. His job was done, he merely hoped that the court would deliver the right verdict. Guilty!

Martyn Wylde looked up, nodded. He turned towards the guards at the door. 'Bring forth the witness.'

Kent stiffened. There were no witnesses. If there had been, then they were already dead. Murdered to keep their silence.

The court waited and fidgeted. The monk had to be supported or else he would have fallen from his stool.

Footsteps receded, somewhere a door opened, closed again. Muttered voices, then the footfalls returned and the oaken door crashed back to admit. . .

Nicholas the coney-catcher.

Kent started. He scarcely believed what his tired eyes saw. Perhaps he had dozed and dreamed. Nicholas had always been a slick dresser but never so natty as today. Such fine silk and velvet was beyond the means even of his thieving fingers and honeyed tongue. The other strutted with an arrogance that was far from his furtive nature.

'Let the witness speak on oath.'

Nicholas spoke with a confidence which had not been there previously, almost an elation. He told how on the night of the robbery he had chanced to be sleeping in close proximity to the church when he had been awakened by the fearful vocal noises of Ned the Beggar. Ned had fled as if a thousand devils were after him, and in his wake came the moonmen. Possibly they did not trust their lookout and were intending to silence him.

Curious, Nicholas had followed at a distance, trailed the men into the forest where, in a clearing lit by moonlight, a cowled man awaited their coming. A moonbeam had chanced to slant on to the stranger's face and Nicholas recognised him, without any possible doubt, as Edmund, the homeless monk.

The sacks which the moonmen bore were loaded on to a hand cart and, with considerable difficulty, Edmund began to wheel it away in the direction of Guy's Cliff. A Herculean task for one man. but the monk was strong, having walked the roads for many years. The gang of robbers, meantime, set off in the opposite direction, presumably with the intention of laying a false trail should there be pursuit.

Nicholas confessed, with affected shame, that he had not followed either the monk or the moonmen, fearing for his life if he was discovered. He wished now that he had trailed the former, for then he would have been able to inform the court where the booty was hidden.

And had the witness seen either the moonmen or the accused since?

Yes, the moonmen when they were brought into town by the constables. The monk. . . Yes, hesitantly, abashed, he hung his head.

Where?

As the court may understand — Nicholas stared down at the floor and his cheeks were flushed — a man who travels the roads and has no wife to share his bed is sometimes tempted by. . . the pleasures of the flesh. One day, the day before yesterday, in fact, the urge was upon him, and hearing that Jane, the whore, had been released from her. . . interrogation, he had made his way to her cottage. Upon entering her garden, he had heard screams from within her cottage and, frightened, he had hidden in the bushes. Shortly afterwards the monk had emerged in a state of extreme agitation; he had passed within a yard of where Nicholas crouched.

Nicholas had not looked inside the cottage, he was too afraid. He feared that if he left by the road, and was seen, whatever had happened inside the cottage might be attributed to himself. So he

71

had climbed through into the adjacent field, and was on the point of running away, when he heard somebody coming.

Nicholas paused in the midst of his embarrassed narrative, turned towards the seats where the public were allowed to sit during trials.

'The man who had arrived at the whore's dwelling,' his voice quavered, his trembling finger pointed to where a green-clad man sat and listened intently, shaking his head from side to side periodically, 'was *him!*'

'Kent,' the churchwarden's voice cut through the murmurs from all around, 'do you admit to having been in the vicinity of the whore's cottage at that time, and did you see this man there?'

'I admit to both.' Kent half rose. 'As you well know, it was I who—'

'Thank you!'

There were whispered mutterings from all around. The jury were glancing expectantly at one another.

'The evidence is damning.' Roland Packard spoke louder now, his eyes sparkling with a sudden zest. 'The whore was found hanged, the monk was seen leaving her cottage. I put it to you that the deceased woman was a witch and involved in the plot, perhaps the monk was in her power. Or else she had discovered his involvement. Whichever is irrelevant. Suffice that the monk, named Edmund, murdered her. We already have the robber's confession which implicated him. I ask you, Jury of Tenants, is this man guilty of witchcraft and murder? Ponder upon the facts given to you, and let me have your verdict.'

Guy Kent trembled with silent anger. Nicholas, the trickster, had turned the tables for them, involved Kent in his evidence. There was no disputing the coney-catcher's presence at Jane's cottage, likewise Edmund had been there also. And who had bought Nicholas his fine clothing?

Kent buried his face in his hands. There was only one possible outcome. *Guilty of witchcraft, robbery and murder.*

The punishment – execution. Doubtless by burning, he reflected grimly. A couple of years ago he had witnessed the burning of a witch in Leamington. A senile hag, they had dragged her screaming to the stake. She yelled abuse, obscenities, at her executioners; one of them slipped a noose around her neck. In some instances death was merciful, as a strong man pulled and broke her neck before the flames began to burn her flesh. She was dead long before her body incinerated.

Kent doubted whether such mercy would be shown towards Edmund in view of the seriousness of the charges against him.

Guilty!

Kent thought that Victor Gask's rendering of his fellows' verdict to the justices of the peace was echoed by Martyn Wylde; it might have been the Witchfinder behind unable to control his euphoric relief. A cheer from the onlookers was taken up by the crowds outside who had listened with bated breath for a sign that they would have their enjoyment.

'. . . taken from this court forthwith, and burned until your body is ashes!'

Kent's pulses raced, his heart stepped up a beat. His fingernails gouged his clammy palms. Lies, faked evidence by a bribed witness. It was all that he could do to stop himself from leaping up and shouting. But it would have done him no good. Certainly it would have had no bearing upon the monk's fate.

The constable supporting the slouched monk stepped back, signalled to his colleagues to help him drag the unfortunate outside to the waiting death cart. At least a burning spared the gravediggers toil in such hot weather.

That was when Edmund fell backwards, hit the floor with a resounding thud.

'He's fainted at the verdict.' The churchwarden leaned forward. 'Revive him. A pail of cold water is as good as anything,'

A constable dropped to one knee, heaved the inert bulk so that it rolled over. Edmund's blood-streaked features were clay white, his swollen mouth fell open. His eyes stared up from out of puffed and blackened sockets. If he saw, then he gave no sign.

The officer lifted the shaven head, let it fall back again.

'Sir,' a note of alarm, almost a cry of despair for there had not been a witch-burning here for many years, *'I. . . the monk is dead!'*

CHAPTER TEN

Cornelius was of stocky build and swarthy skin, with a bulbous nose that might at some stage in his life have been broken; thick lips and bushy eyebrows gave the appearance of coarseness. An indeterminable age was possibly due to the balding of his crown although his long side locks were as raven as they had been in youth. Two large gold earrings hung heavy from his lobes, seemed to pull them down. Multicoloured attire, his dark brown skin was cleaner than that of most townspeople for he bathed unclothed in stream or river every day of the year even if it was necessary to break the ice to do so.

His father, and his grandfather, before him had led these Romanies on their travels throughout the length and breadth of the country. Often persecuted, they seldom retaliated, preferring to go their own way in peace to quieter pastures. Now the Welcombe Hills were no place to linger. Villainy and witchcraft were all around. The much-feared Witchfinder had been deprived of a burning, would surely look for another.

Stratford was not as it had once been. Cornelius had tried to explain that, with great difficulty, to the younger generation of gypsies. He spoke of a time when few from afar came here, and people who lived further than Warwick or Leamington had not even heard of this town. Then some scribe had begun writing plays that were performed in London and now folks travelled here to see where he lived, turned it into some kind of shrine. Far better, would it not have been, to let the travelling players perform his plays in his home town and not encourage Londoners here? For Cornelius had passed through London on his travels and it was no safe place to stay, teeming with footpads and tricksters.

'Ned?' Cornelius hooded his heavy eyebrows with suspicion. 'Why is everybody so concerned because Ned came here that night? We turned him away. His wanderings are no business of ours. We only ask to be left in peace.'

'Who else has enquired about Ned the Beggar?' Guy Kent eyed the gypsy leader shrewdly.

'The Witchfinder asked. The constable was with him. Another fellow too – lean and hungry looking, wide breeches and an even wider hat.'

'That would be Martyn Wylde, the churchwarden.'

'Aye. They were looking for the moonmen, too, and I'm glad that they caught them else they might have blamed us for that foul deed. Romanies are all too often scapegoats for the crimes of vagabonds.'

'Where did Ned go when he left here?' Kent asked the question casually; gypsies were a close-knit community, and seldom volunteered information to outsiders. 'Maybe everybody has their different reasons for wanting to know that. I have mine, and they in no way involve the Romanies.'

'He sought and found shelter with the whore. She told us so, she walked these woods often and sometimes stopped to talk with us. Now they've killed her, too.'

Kent caught his breath, his pulses quickened. Ned had spent the night with Jane, maybe slept in her porch. Whores had hearts of gold, harmed none, and were greatly maligned by Church hypocrites. 'I see.' He tried to appear unconcerned. 'Then I fail to understand what all the fuss is about.'

'The monk came here, too. It's best I tell you so as to save you the trouble of coming back again to ask.' Cornelius spat on the ground. 'We refused to allow him to travel with us, either. We wanted none of his praying and preaching. We have our own beliefs and they have nothing to do with churches nor monasteries. Besides, Catholics and Protestants are always feuding, no matter how the Queen might try to change all that. We do not want to be seen to be taking sides in religious quarrels; it was best that the monk, like the beggar, went his own way. Gypsies are gypsies, we keep to ourselves. When the likes of you and your people will let us, that is.' He spat again.

'The monk's dead, too,' Kent watched the other carefully as he spoke.

'I know.'

'How do you know?'

'Gypsies know most things.' Suspicion flickered in those dark eyes. 'We see and hear but we don't interfere.'

'They tortured and tried him for witchcraft and murder.' Kent's voice was terse; he made no attempt to conceal the anger which smouldered inside him. 'He would not confess, defied them right up to the end. He died in court – at least they did not have the satisfaction of burning him. The pain and stress were too much for him. He had a seizure.'

'Well, it is no business of ours.' Cornelius shrugged, turned away. 'We must be moving on. We are the last to leave; I wanted to see the others safely on their way before I followed. The Locks left yesterday.'

'Your fortune, sir?' A hunched and wizened woman appeared in the doorway of the red and yellow caravan, peered from beneath an oversize green headscarf, her body swathed in a capacious shawl in spite of the heat. 'You have a lucky face, sir.'

'Woman, you waste time when we should be on our way,' Cornelius growled. 'This is no place to tarry.' His hairy nostrils flared. 'Even now I scent death in the air. Pray that it will not be ours!'

'It will not take long to tell this young man what life holds for him.' She was undeterred, saliva stringing from her toothless gums.

Kent watched her clamber down the wooden steps, clutching the rail as she came. She was undoubtedly very old.

'Raol is the best fortune teller on the roads.' The Romany leader's attitude had changed; there was a note of pride in his voice. 'Nevertheless, hurry, for we must be gone from here.'

She took Kent's hand and her callused fingers prised open his own, her head bent forward to examine his palm. 'A long life, sir, maybe even longer than mine. Troubled, too, but you will overcome your difficulties. I see danger but you will not be harmed.' She looked up into his face. 'These are troubled times for us all but they will get better. You've a woman, sir, but she is not your wife, perhaps will never be.'

Kent stiffened. She had probably heard from others, strollers in the woods, or else it was shrewd guesswork based on his love-locks.

'You are very perceptive,' he said, humouring her.

'She has died recently.'

He went cold instantly, snatched his hand free. 'No, she was fine when I left her less than an hour ago.'

'No, I refer to another for whom you secretly grieve, one who met an untimely death a short time ago.'

Jane! Thank God! The gypsies knew Jane because she frequently rambled in the woods. 'Tell me something new, not gossip and hearsay.'

Raol appeared not to have heard him. Her eyes were closed, her pouted lips dribbled as they moved silently as though she communed with the unseen. Kent's uneasiness grew. Cornelius had moved away, gone behind the caravan as if he wished to have no part in this.

'She was murdered.'

Kent swallowed. The ground beneath him seemed to tilt slightly; instinctively he clutched at the old gypsy woman for support.

'Hanged, but not on the gallows.'

Damn it, everybody knew that, it had come up at Edmund's trial when the monk was accused of killing Jane. The town had been packed with expectant crowds, those inside the court had heard the evidence, they had whispered it out in the streets. It was no wonder that it had travelled as far as the gypsy encampment.

'I see her struggling.' Raol's features were contorted, her hands went up to her neck as though she, too, suffered the agonies of the rope. She was shaking and her voice was a scarcely audible whisper. 'A man. . . I cannot see him properly, the light is too dim. Now he has her. . . she is too weak to resist, the rope is around her neck!' She was pulling at her own neck as if she was trying to loosen a constricting, strangling hempen noose. 'It is thrown over a beam. He forces her to clamber up on to a footstool. He kicks it away, the rope tautens. . . *she hangs!*'

Raol screamed, fell writhing to the ferny floor.

Guy Kent, fearing that the woman had suffered a seizure, dropped on to his knees by her side. A bundle of coloured rags with a face peeping out of them, eyes closed; she barely seemed to breathe.

'She will be all right.' Cornelius had appeared silently, towering above Kent. There was no trace of concern on his features. Instead, a hint of a smile; he might even have been expecting this to happen. 'It occurs from time to time when she speaks with the dead. It is too much for her but she suffers no harm other than a faint. The worst that happens is that she frightens strangers. And that is no bad thing,' he growled.

Raol's lips began to move. Kent bent and put his ear against them in an attempt to catch her words.

'Jane is. . . trying to speak to me.' The old woman shook, clutched the air with her claw-like hands.

The icy tingling that had begun at the base of Kent's spine travelled right up to the nape of his neck, prickled its way on up into his scalp. 'Ask her. . . *ask her the name of the man who hanged her!*'

Raol did not appear to hear him. Her features contorted almost beyond recognition, then relaxed. Her trembling ceased, her arms fell by her sides. 'She is lifeless now, her soul has left her body.'

'Can you not see this man clearer now?'

There was no answer.

Kent glanced up, saw that Cornelius was walking away, satisfied that no ill had befallen his woman. Communion with the dead, it appeared, was nothing to become excited about.

'*Her soul speaks to me now.*' Raol's voice was louder. She had tensed again.

'Ask her. . .'

A hand crippled with rheumatism bade him be silent. 'She says. . .'

'Yes?'

'She asks for one named. . . *Guy.*'

'That's me.'

'She speaks. . .' There was a moment of silence before Raol continued. *'The eyes of the deaf and dumb are keenest of all.'*

It might have been an echo within his own mind, torturing him. He forced himself to wait patiently.

'An old beggar man, he told her. . .' The gypsy gave the impression that she was straining to catch words from beyond the grave that were fast fading. 'He saw. . . recognised. . .'

'Whom? Tell me whom old Ned recognised?' Kent was unable to contain himself any longer, his words spilling out in an unstoppable rush.

Raol jerked as if in a falling dream. Only the whites of her eyes were visible. It was like looking down upon the blind. Or the dead.

Then, slowly, the pupils dropped back down and she met his gaze, reproach but not anger in her tired eyes. 'You broke the contact by your chatter, sir.'

Kent bit on his lip until he tasted blood. His impatience had been his own undoing. 'I'm sorry.'

'It matters not to me.' Raol smiled. 'I did not ask to speak with the one who calls herself Jane. I just happened, by chance, to make contact with her whilst searching for your fortune, sir. She was waiting there, now she is gone. It would be better had I not spoken with her at all.'

'Can you not call her back?'

'No. The dead are reluctant to return once a discourse is broken. Next time it will be somebody else. It becomes tiresome talking with strangers, your concentration goes. Often, you never hear from them again.'

So near yet so far. Kent curbed his frustration. Of course, Raol might have been bluffing – many of the roaming fortune-tellers were fakes, seeking a coin on their palm in return for fictitious glad tidings. But Raol's exhaustion, her trembling, belied this.

'I need to know the name of the one who hanged Jane.' Because it was undoubtedly he who had stolen from the church and murdered old Ned. The killer's identity had almost been within Kent's grasp, then it was snatched away. For ever.

'Some white heather to bring you luck, sir.' She held out a sprig. 'Methinks that you will need luck if you are to succeed. Problems beset you but they will be overcome with perseverance and bravery.'

'Thank you.'

An upraised hand refused a monetary reward. In her own

estimation, Raol had failed. 'Remember the beggar's words, sir, as conveyed to us by Jane, for the afflicted are often more observant than such as us. Jane is attempting to warn you. Beware him whom the beggar saw for he hanged her for her knowledge. *Just as he will kill you for yours. Even now he plots your death.*'

Kent was disturbed as he rode back towards Stratford. He was no nearer a solution than he had been a week ago, but now, suddenly, the hunter had become the hunted.

CHAPTER ELEVEN

'He will not survive the night.' Rhys, the aged physician, paused on the stairs, whispered to the churchwarden. 'Indeed, the poor fellow may not even see the hour out. It is just a question of when the Lord calls him. The stroke which we feared he might have suffered on discovering that Satan had entered the church, and gave thanks that it was not so, has now taken him. The Reverend Long flits in and out of consciousness; ere long he will sleep and not awake.'

'It matters not if I disturb him, then?'

Deformed shoulders shrugged. 'Ultimately, no. But should he not be allowed to rest in his final hours?'

'Soon, according to what you say, he will rest long enough.' Wylde pushed past the other. 'Do not worry, I will not outstay my welcome. I have a matter pertaining to the Church which he may yet still be lucid enough to discuss with me, but I think he would die happier knowing that those who defiled God's house have been caught and punished, even if the monk did cheat his executioners at the last.'

The parson blended with the whiteness of his bedclothes, eyes closed and mouth agape, only his rasping breath a sign that he still clung to life. Beside him on the small bedside table rested a pitcher of water and a drinking vessel wherewith to quench his raging thirst; he had not eaten for four days. Most likely the cleric would die thirsting, Wylde thought as he stood just inside the doorway, for he would not have the strength to lift a drink up to his lips. Possibly he would not even regain consciousness and the journey here would have been a waste of time.

Even as Martyn Wylde watched, the figure in the bed stirred, muttered something that was unintelligible and barely audible. Then his eyelids opened as if he sensed a presence in the curtained bedroom, and he stared with hollowed and red-rimmed eyes.

'Churchwarden, is it perchance you?' A cracked voice but at least he was coherent; either he recognised the visitor to his deathbed or else he had anticipated the coming of the churchwarden.

'Indeed it is, Reverend. I called to see how you fared, to bring good news as well as bad tidings, although the latter may not be as bad as we feared. The villains have been punished, but although their booty has not yet been found, if the constables are successful in their search we may yet unearth the missing artefacts. I remain optimistic.'

'That is marvellous news for supposedly bad tidings!' Long seemed to revive, found the strength to lift himself up on to an elbow. 'I can go to the Lord with the satisfaction of knowing that those who defiled His church have been brought to book. And their punishment?' The sunken eyes glinted in anticipation, for the bishop had decreed that no mercy be shown towards witches, and the will of the bishop was the will of God.

'The culprits, witches and robbers, have been executed after a fair trial. A bunch of moonmen, commanded by a cunning monk who might never have been in holy orders. Another accomplice, a whore, was murdered by him, as was the beggar. Apart from the rediscovery of the artefacts, the whole matter has been brought to a satisfactory conclusion, I am pleased to report. And I hear from Rhys that you will soon be from your bed and about again.' He spoke the lie with conviction, smiled confidently. 'Exhaustion and a fever, and it is no wonder after recent events. You must not try to hasten your convalescence, though.'

'You lie, churchwarden, but with the best of intentions.' Long managed a smile. 'I shall be with God ere long, for in His mercy He sees fit not to leave me helpless on this earth where I should be but a burden to others who might serve Him more usefully. It is the will of the Lord. Amen.'

Long's eyes closed once more. The effort of talking had exhausted him; he might even have fallen asleep again. Wylde moved a couple of paces nearer, saw how the other's lips blew in time with his laboured breathing.

'Reverend?'

It was some moments before those reddened eyelids lifted again, disturbed from the beginning of a long sleep. 'Yes?'

'There is another matter on which I hesitate to trouble you, but I feel that I must ask your guidance for it is a matter pertaining to parish affairs, and does not the Church control the parish?'

'Indeed it does.' The parson's eyelids drooped but curiosity prevailed over the desire for sleep. 'What is it that you wish to ask my advice about, churchwarden?'

'A matter concerning parish funds, Reverend.' Wylde hesitated, perhaps questioning his own lack of wisdom in approaching the parson on his deathbed.

'Yes, yes. Go on.'

The churchwarden took a deep breath, let it out slowly. 'I believe that there has been a misappropriation of parochial funds, Reverend.'

'I. . .' The parson's eyelids lifted but he had difficulty in recovering his weakening power of speech. '*Parochial* funds, you say, churchwarden. Then is that not a matter for Matthew King, the parish clerk, who is also accountable to the Church?'

'It is as you say, Reverend, but I considered it only courteous to speak with you first for it is a matter of extreme delicacy. As you are aware, I am authorised to make an infrequent check of the ledger, in the same way that I am required to sample the ale in all the ale houses and inns to ensure that all is well. On the afternoon following the trial of the perpetrators of the church robbery, I made an unannounced call at the office of the parish clerk. He was away collecting taxes at Snitterfield at the time so I took the liberty of examining the ledgers in his absence. Much to my chagrin, I discovered a discrepancy of some magnitude. Of course, it may be merely a mathematical error that can be rectified with the stroke of a pen. . .'

'May God preserve us!' Long somehow found the strength to raise himself up a second time. 'Another robbery! First the church silver and gold, now the revenue from taxation and tithes.'

'Just taxation, so far, and, as I said, I shall instigate a recheck with Matthew King.' Wylde fidgeted with his long fingers. 'However, I am only able to check the taxes received. The tithes, which are the Church's responsibility although King collects them, are kept under your own control. I wonder if I may browse through the ledger in question? I hope that it is in order, but I need to be very thorough in my checking before I speak with the parish clerk. I have never had need to scrutinise your ledger before but I thought, whilst you are unwell, I could compare the amount quoted with what the parish clerk has transferred to the taxation account. However, I fear that I am right and that for some reason, even if it is an accounting or mathematical error, the parish clerk has not drawn my attention to it. Perhaps he hopes to rectify the shortfall before my next check.'

'Are you. . .' Samuel Long's wasted features were aghast; there was no way in which he could withstand further shock. 'Do you mean that. . . that Matthew King has been misappropriating parochial funds for his personal misuse, churchwarden?'

'I have no proof at the moment, and I would not accuse anybody until I am certain. But suffice that the figures do not tally with the revenue collected. Perhaps a transfer has been made to the tithes ledger and not recorded in the revenue one, I cannot say until I peruse the records.'

'The ledger is on the lower shelf in my study, on the far right. You cannot miss it. Please take it with you, churchwarden, and let us both pray that this whole business is a mistake, that the only blame to be apportioned is that for carelessness. I, myself, may be at fault, although during this last year I have allowed Mister King to take away the ledger and do the accounting. I trusted him – I still do. I cannot believe that. . .'

'Let us not pre-judge, Reverend, until I have checked and rechecked.'

'I have neglected the responsibility bestowed upon me by the bishop in allowing, and trusting, another to undertake a duty which is rightfully mine. It is *I* who am guilty, for I have laid temptation before another. If there has been theft, only access to both ledgers would permit the falsification of both sets of figures, thereby rendering it undetectable except by the shrewdest of men!' The parson's voice was shrill in his self-recrimination.

'I was elected churchwarden on the premise of my shrewdness,' Wylde replied, unabashed. 'Consequently, I thought it advisable to speak with you at this early stage, even though you suffer a temporary bout of ill health, so that the matter can be concluded as swiftly as possible. In the extreme unlikelihood of a fraud's having been committed – and I have always found Matthew King to be honest and diligent in his duties – then I must report it to the Lord Lieutenant and the bishop in Warwick, and request that a higher authority than mine arbitrates. We must, however, avert a scandal which would be damaging to the Church at a time when our Queen seeks harmony between Catholics and Protestants.'

The Reverend Long sank back on to his pillow. His lips moved but no sound came from them. He had exhausted the strength which necessity had afforded him. He stared straight ahead, unseeing, unhearing. His eyelids slowly closed and his head sagged to one side.

Martyn Wylde remained until the shadows on the wall began to lengthen and the other's features were no longer discernible. Only then did he creep softly away, pausing downstairs to find the ledger of which he had need. He smiled to himself in the gloom of the hallway, anticipating with some relish his confrontation with Matthew King. For the churchwarden was entering the twilight of his term of office and shortly the powers bestowed upon him would be rescinded. And he was a man who craved power. He would miss it dearly.

Outside, he closed the door behind him, breathed in the warm freshness of a summer's night, allowed it to permeate his lungs, for he was only too familiar with that unmistakable odour of death.

He would leave it to Rhys, the physician, to pronounce the parson dead.

'On the face of it, the matter seems to have been concluded, even if that conclusion leave us both with a sense of dissatisfaction.' Richard ap Cynon stood looking out of the window across the parkland as was his wont when he did not wish a visitor to read his expression.

'Apparently so, my lord.' Kent watched apprehensively. He knew only too well those signs which indicated the Lord Lieutenant's unease: the fidgeting of the hands clasped just a shade too tightly behind the back, a booted foot tapping irritatingly on the floor. A turmoil of indecision seethed inside the one who had the power to make decisions throughout the county.

'There is really no reason for you to remain in Stratford further, Kent.' A statement of fact that lacked conviction.

'No, my lord, none at all.'

'No reason at all.' Repetition was a sure sign of contradiction where Richard ap Cynon was concerned. 'The monk killed the beggar in the stocks to silence him, hanged the whore for the same reason. The moonmen robbed the church and have been executed for their crime, and the monk has died of a seizure. Our questions have been answered. Unsatisfactorily.'

'Most unsatisfactorily, my lord.'

'Which is why I wish you to remain in Stratford for a little while longer, Kent. Perhaps a couple of weeks, no more. I had it in mind to despatch you to Atherstone, where a tenant farmer's wife has died from what seems to be hemlock poisoning; rumour has it that the farmer has a young and comely mistress, and one or the other of them has possibly poisoned the wife. Still, the business will keep. Neither the farmer nor his mistress will run away, and whichever is guilty – or both – will hang equally well next month as next week. I fear, though, that this beggar's death has besmirched the reputation of our judicial system. Do the common folk really believe the monk to be a witch and a murderer?'

'They were eager enough for a witch-burning, sir. Disappointment was widespread at the news of his untimely death from natural causes.'

'In which case it would be a good thing to prove the monk's innocence, perhaps prick their consciences. If they have consciences! They are no better than the Witchfinder, revelling in torture and death, caring nothing for justice. A victim is sufficient regardless of whether he is guilty or innocent. Now the Witchfinder's appetite is temporarily satisfied, he has returned to Derbyshire to complete unfinished business there. Warwickshire witches will either flee or lie low after this latest purge. In time they will return or surface; witchcraft will never be eradicated, no matter how optimistic is the Church. My priority at this time is for justice to be seen to be done. I fear that witchcraft has sidetracked us from the main issue, a scent that has thrown off the hounds, including yourself, Kent. The entire business, to my thinking, stinks of a fabrication.'

'And to mine, sir.'

'I am glad our instincts are mutual. We may be wasting our time. The crime, like the criminals, is dead and buried, the church artefacts gone for ever, smelted down by some London smith of dubious reputation in return for a groat or two. Yet my inner feelings urge me to persevere for a little while longer yet. Because, possibly, somewhere, there is some hitherto undiscovered factor which will throw a different meaning on to everything that has gone before. It may already have stared us in the face but we have been blind to it. Or it may be so cunningly concealed that we shall never find it.'

'I will return to Stratford, my lord.'

'Good!' Richard ap Cynon turned round and Kent saw that the lines on his handsome features seemed to be etched deeper than before. 'Dig deep, but in a secretive fashion, for who knows what corruption lurks beneath the cloak of respectability, what you may uncover that makes the beggar's death a trivial incident in a web of intrigue, something which even the bard himself has not thought up for one of his plays? There are insidious rumours circulating amongst society that his plays are written for him by another. Such a revelation would destroy the spreading fame of Stratford, make a mockery of us all. Deceit has no boundaries, Kent, no social barriers.' He laughed like a court fool who had jested and, receiving no response, provided his own mirth in an attempt to cover up a *faux pas*. 'Of course, I only quote an extreme example to illustrate my point, do not take it literally.' He turned back to the window again to hide his expression.

An uneasy silence followed. It seemed an embarrassing eternity before the Lord Lieutenant spoke again.

'Kent?'

'Sir?'

'I hesitate to send you back to Stratford, none the less, not because of what scandal irrelevant to a beggar's murder you may uncover, not just because it might be a futile attempt to solve a non-existent mystery which has become almost an obsession with me for the sake of my reputation. But for another reason.'

Kent waited, curious.

'I fear for your very safety, Kent, if you pursue this dark business further, when others believe that it is closed and they breathe sighs of relief.' There was no doubting the concern in the other's expression when he turned back. 'Murder is not finished with yet, I fear. Carry a pistol at all times and be doubly watchful of those around you. Trust none, for they who kill beggars and whores will not hesitate to murder an envoy of the Lord Lieutenant who attempts to sniff out their closely guarded dark secrets; when perchance his investigations might bring to light a plot of such cunning and evil that the perpetrators would go to the gallows. As I say, I hesitate to send you, but who else will scent out the evil that spawns in Stratford before it is too late?'

CHAPTER TWELVE

Edward Las had only vague memories of his upbringing in London and he preferred not to recall them, for they were not pleasant.

Shortly after Edward was born his father had died, the victim of a summer outbreak of typhus fever, and his mother was left to bring up their nine children; Edward was unable to remember the names of all his brothers and sisters; of whom two had died in infancy and the eldest, John, was found drowned in the Thames.

His mother sent him out on to the streets to beg for food but he soon discovered that it was easier to steal. Other ragged urchins taught him how to snatch food from market stalls, to run the gauntlet of a forest of hands that tried to grab him by his threadbare shirt, to dive between outstretched legs and to overturn barrows of fruit in order to hinder his pursuers. Street thieves were an accepted part of life in the capital, and the constables did not go to any great lengths to apprehend them, preferring to concentrate upon the footpads who lurked in dark alleyways and constituted a threat to the gentry going about their business. Prisons and orphanages were overflowing; far better to leave it to Nature to cull this human pestilence with her constant outbreaks of disease.

Edward's small stature, never fully developed in later life due to poor nutrition in infancy, was an advantage to his thieving. His mother, a fearsome woman of large build, gathered her remaining children in their single-roomed hovel each evening and demanded that they hand over whatever they had managed to acquire during the day by quickness of hand and fleetness of foot, to be shared amongst them all. Woe betide any of them who returned empty-handed; her fist was heavy and the unfortunate was cuffed and sent to bed with an empty belly on a heap of unwashed blankets.

There were, however, a few pleasant interludes in this existence of seemingly eternal destitution: the slaughtering of cocks at Shrovetide, games of handball played at Easter for tansy cakes, the rope-bindings of Hock Tuesday and, of course, Christmas, which was a chaos of fun and mischief. But, whilst the pickings in the city were rich, the numbers of thieves were increasing, and, thus, Edward progressed from common theft to the art of the footpad. He learned his trade from observing the notorious Ally (so named because of the areas in which he plied his trade) who, in due course, ended his career of robbery with excessive violence on the end of a rope on Tyburn hill.

Nevertheless, it was a far more lucrative way of life than pilfering from the markets; the risks were greater but all that was required was a strong arm to wield a heavy cudgel.

But Edward lacked the brute strength and experience of his unwitting mentor. He took to wielding his weapon with both hands and a clumsy blow on an unprotected skull, delivered with a lack of expertise, can kill a man instantly. Which was what occurred on Edward's second bungled robbery (on the first his victim's purse was discovered to be empty) and, with the constables hunting a murderer, he fled London and headed north.

Reverting to his former cunning in the manner of thieving, he eventually came into possession of a firearm, a fine specimen of a miquelet belt pistol, exquisitely engraved and inlaid with gold, which he took from an inebriated trader one night outside an inn. Edward might have obtained a fair price for it but it seemed sacrilege to part with it. Likewise, it was a weapon of such magnificence that it was tempting to display it with pride. However, Edward's limited discretion prevailed and he carried it belted beneath his travelling coat.

Unbelievably, he discovered that he had a talent for marksmanship; he learned to hit not only the trunk of an oak at twenty paces but a chosen bough. His skill developed with practice so that sometimes he was able to shred a sprouting leaf at the same distance with five shots out of ten.

The pistol gave him a feeling of power over his more fortunate fellows. A travelling tradesman on a lonely road seldom offered any resistance when faced with a levelled pistol, whereas a brave man would sometimes chance his luck against knife or club. Close combat was something which Edward avoided at all times for his early life had stunted his growth and deprived him of physical strength. A weakling who had survived, against all odds, the ravages of poverty and disease, he developed a bitterness towards the society which had made him what he was.

He saw in his new skill a means whereby to earn a handsome living, whilst at the same time exacting revenge upon those in more fortunate circumstances than his own. Thus, on his arrival in Oxfordshire, he embarked upon the precarious occupation of highway robbery.

It was not as simple, nor as lucrative, as he had at first believed. Often a long wait on a deserted stretch of road ended with not seeing anybody throughout the tedious vigil. Victims had to be chosen with some discrimination; a yeoman or tenant farmer exercising his horse, or merely out riding for pleasure, was unlikely to be carrying money or valuables. Edward learned this on his first hold-up, a barren episode which resulted in his having to move on to another area because the constables were scouring the woods for him. Messengers delivering mail between market towns seldom had anything other than letters in their saddle pouches, and challenging more than two travellers was an unwarranted risk when one only had a single shot to call upon. A lone gentleman was a rarity; mostly they rode in company for safety reasons.

He fashioned a domino mask out of a piece of waste velvet and wore a cloak to hide his recognisable peasant garb. A mount would have been to his advantage; perhaps he might purchase one at a later stage when he had accumulated capital. In the meantime, he relied upon dense woodlands to hide him when the alarm was raised.

It was in Banbury that he had his first fortuitous experience, one that he happened upon on a visit to an ale house. A young man of yeoman class was becoming steadily drunk, entertaining the other drinkers with ribald stories and graphic accounts of his recent affair with the wife of an esquire. It seemed, from snatches of conversation which Edward overheard, that the latter had challenged his rival to a duel with pistols at daybreak the next morning on some nearby common land. And judging by the state of the yeoman it would be a 'no contest', the highwayman reflected.

The young adulterer produced his unprimed pistol, a weapon that was obviously too weighty and unbalanced for duelling, which required a swift and steady hand, and proceeded to rehearse his role in the forthcoming event. He lost his footing and fell headlong, much to the amusement of his audience.

Some time later, when most of the revellers had gone home to their beds, the drunken yeoman fell into conversation with the highwayman. Gone was the former's bravado; he realised only too well the seriousness of the gauntlet which he had rashly picked up. He could, of course, back down but family pride was at stake. His lean features took on a shifty expression and he lowered his voice; the squire would arrive at the pre-arranged destination just as the birds began their morning chorus. Now, if an unscrupulous and able marksman happened to be concealed in the bushes close by, 'and you, sir, seem to be the man I am looking for. . .' A bag of coins was produced, jangled. Las nodded; he had the gist of what was expected of him. And there would be a further payment on completion of the assignment. The squire was unlikely to bring a second with him for the matter was one of extreme delicacy and he would have no wish to create a scandal. He would be presuming that his opponent would capitulate without ever a shot being fired.

Edward Las was in place before daybreak, the yeoman arrived shortly afterwards and within minutes the hoofbeats of the approaching squire vibrated the ground. Las shot him as he dismounted, a feat of which he was duly proud, the ball smashing the other's forehead and dropping him instantly. With the integrity expected of a gentleman whose honour has been preserved, the young yeoman handed the highwayman the promised second instalment of his reward for the service rendered, and that should have been the end of the matter.

Unfortunately for the yeoman, it was not. Duelling was against the law and he was arrested by the constable for murder. At his trial he pleaded his innocence, claimed that it was not he who had fired the fatal ball but some rascal whom he had met at the inn the night before and duly persuaded to second him. An examination of his pistol proved the defendant's point but he was subsequently found guilty of inciting and being an accessary to murder, and hanged.

A warrant was issued for the arrest of Edward Las but the highwayman fled north to Warwickshire, well satisfied with the twenty pounds with which he had been paid, a sum that enabled him to live in a manner which did not attract the attention of the law whilst the hunt was still on for him.

But Edward Las had established his notoriety as both highwayman and hired assassin. A reward was offered for information leading to his arrest. Consequently, the County of Warwickshire was uneasy at the knowledge that he was at large within its boundaries, and churchwardens alerted their constabulary to be on the lookout for him.

The urchin snatch thief from Hackney had become a man to be feared.

Talbot Christie and Edgar Ridge had remained overnight in Stratford following the trial of the moonmen and Edmund the homeless monk. Far better, they decided, to obtain a good night's sleep and make a fresh start on the hazardous journey early the next morning, for it was dangerous to be abroad on lonely roads; one of their horses might cast a shoe and delay them into darkness.

So they rose early the next morning and breakfasted heartily on venison pasty with sugared mustard and roasted pears, washed down with strong cider. Such fare fortified men for the most arduous of journeys, the ostler informed them as he led their saddled mounts out of the stables.

Christie was tall and lean, a taciturn man whose moods often influenced the other justices of the peace. Ridge was short and stocky; he had an inexhaustible repertoire of bawdy stories but he knew the company in which to recount them. He would not be telling any today.

'We should make it well before dark.' Christie checked that the pistol was still in the saddle holster. There was an edginess about him.

'Aye, and that allows time for some refreshment on the way.' Ridge grinned. 'It will be a thirsty ride even taking it steady.'

'The churchwarden has done little about road repairs this year.' The taller man stared disparagingly at the dried-up potholes. 'A horse could easily break a leg, throw its rider. I shall see that the Lord Lieutenant knows about this. It's a disgrace. The fellow spends too much time testing the ale and not enough on other duties.'

'And who can blame him?' Ridge controlled his instinctive guffaw. 'If ever I'm elected, Talbot, the ale will take priority!'

'The man has his qualities.' Humour was lost on Talbot Christie. 'A devout churchman and lawman, I admire him for that. But I care less for the constable, Symes. A shifty fellow, if ever there was one.'

'I'll second that, and I'll wager there's many a groat touches his palm in exchange for a look in the opposite direction. But they say he's the nemesis of beggars, that the day will come when there won't be one to be seen on the streets of Stratford, and that's no bad thing.'

'Then why go to all the trouble to try to find who killed one? A crime, but it did the town a favour. Ought not the constable to be out looking for this highwayman?' Talbot Christie's hand rested on the butt of his pistol. He glanced behind, peered at a clump of elders that wilted by the roadside. 'The law demands that all saplings and undergrowth growing alongside roads are cut down so that they cannot hide felons. There are enough bushes on this stretch to conceal an army.'

Edgar Ridge fell silent. His companion was an habitual complainer; even the justices at Warwick were tiring of him.

'I hear the bard is invited to join Richard ap Cynon's table next month.' A hint of bitterness. Christie kicked his mount's flanks, hauled on the reins when it started forward. 'I suppose he is of greater importance than the yeomen and tenants who feed the population! One cannot dine on words, but it seems that a writer of plays will not go hungry!'

'Aye, you are right, Talbot. Words are bad for the digestion but they don't fill your belly.'

'What's up with this nag?' Christie pulled on the reins viciously. His horse was shying.

'It does not care for the heat any more than you or I. It is probably thirsty, but all the roadside pools are dry with dust. Perhaps we should rest our mounts in the shade for a while. There are some mighty oaks over there.'

'It is dangerous to dally. We are not at Heath End yet.'

'And we'll still be home long before dusk.'

'Well, for just a short time, then.' He urged the horse in the direction of the tall trees. It shied again, threatened to rear up on its hind legs. 'Damn, pander to a horse and it still isn't satisfied. I'd teach it a lesson and ride it hard were it not for the state of this road. I promise you, Martyn Wylde shall receive a reprimand from the Lord Lieutenant for his negligence even though the fellow has but two months of his term to serve.'

Edgar Ridge's mount was backing off, too. It neighed, its eyes rolling as it stubbornly resisted its rider's attempts to guide it over to the shade of the trees. 'Methinks, Talbot, we'll let these horses sweat, teach 'em a lesson.'

'Something's unnerving them.' The other felt for his pistol.

'Maybe a vagrant sleeping in the heat of the day. In which case we'll continue on our way and—'

A figure emerged from beneath the trees, a small man with an oversize travelling coat wrapped around his sparse frame and a hat that was a size too small for his head with the brim pulled low, perhaps to shade his eyes against the glare of the sun.

'Be damned if you weren't right, Edgar! A vagrant, and doubtless coming to beg from two passing travellers. Use your whip on him, teach him a lesson he won't forget!'

The stranger came towards them with a shambling gait, and it was only when he lifted his head that the two horsemen noticed the domino mask which concealed the upper half of his face. Both had their whips raised in readiness; too late they saw the sunlight glinting on the burnished barrel of the pistol which pointed at them in a hand that was steady and all the more menacing for that.

'Throw down your money and you'll not be harmed, I promise you.'

The horses reared, almost threw their riders. Hands were fully occupied trying to bring them under control; there was no opportunity to draw pistols. But even when they had steadied their horses, both men realised the foolishness of attempting to arm themselves; the robber had only one shot but it was an even bet which one of them would fall wounded, or even dead, from his saddle.

'We carry no money,' Ridge blustered.

'You lie!' The highwayman spoke with an accent foreign to these parts. 'Do I have to take it from a corpse?'

'It's *him!*' Talbot Christie's whisper trembled. 'Edward Las. I recognise him from the drawing on the reward poster, even with his mask.'

Edgar Ridge blanched. There were stories that this man was a paid assassin, murdered for money in cold blood. Other tales, too, that might or might not have been embellished in the telling. They would not take any risk on the authenticity of those alehouse yarns.

'Hurry!'

'All right, we'll give you money.'

'Don't reach for your pistols, the first to do so is dead!'

They did not doubt his threat; his grimed forefinger rested on the trigger. Talbot's shaking hand fumbled in his bag, coins clinked. A purse kicked up a small dust cloud as it hit the road. A second, somewhat heavier, joined it.

'Now ride on. I can drop you at thirty paces and you can't harm me further than that.'

This time the horses did not hesitate. They knew danger when they scented it and plunged forward, their riders clinging on grimly.

Only when the next bend hid them did Edward Las move. He stooped, lifted up the purses, smiled to himself as he felt their weight.

'And may their souls rot if these are full of farthings!' He grunted, shaded his eyes to make sure that the horsemen were not in sight, listened in case they were making a detour behind the oaks to come back upon him.

He nodded his satisfaction when his ears picked up the faint sound of distant hoofbeats. Gentlemen had no stomach for a fight. But he must be far from here by the time they returned with the constables.

CHAPTER THIRTEEN

Constable Bill Symes stood beneath the town hall arches, shaded his eyes against the sunlight with his fleshy hands, stared in obvious disbelief at what he saw on the opposite side of Chapel Street.

'It has to be the heat.' His thick lips moved, his guttural tones addressed to himself. 'Surely 'tis a mirage. Or else I'm dreaming it. What in the name of God is that jackass doing in town? A government spy looking for tales to tell to the Lord Lieutenant, doubtless.'

The constable instinctively stepped back behind a stone pillar, his eyes narrowed furtively. There was a momentary glimmer of fear in them. Had not Guy Kent caused trouble enough already, created suspicion amongst the rabble that the constables were not carrying out their duties, that they needed an overseer?

Symes tensed, would have drawn back still further except that the other had spotted him and was crossing the street, coming towards him. Bill Symes's mouth was suddenly dry and he experienced an urge to empty his bowels. He reproached himself, a grown man with the authority to uphold the law, fearing this whippersnapper who still wore love-locks.

'Good day to you, constable.' Kent's smile was disarming.

'And to you, sir. And what brings you back to Stratford?'

'I like the air here, it is invigorating. Is that not reason enough? I trust all has been well during my absence?'

'As well as can be expected in this heat. The wells are running dry, the outbreak of fever spreads – mostly the poor. The charnel house is full and the gravediggers are working from dawn till dusk to keep pace. And the parson has passed on, too.'

'I'm sorry to learn that,' Kent's smile faded, 'but it was inevitable even before I left.'

'Aye, a seizure at the end.'

'Is the churchwarden around?'

'He's busy, sir. Checking the taxes and tithes. He's give instructions that he's not to be disturbed.'

'Then I shall accede to his request and speak to him later. Tell me, constable, have you seen the coney-catcher?'

'Why?' Suspicion clouded the other's eyes again.

'I wish to talk to him.'

'I have not seen him this last couple of days. I have heard that he left town. He is free to come and go as he pleases. To my knowledge he has committed no crime.'

'A matter of opinion, constable. And was he still wearing his fine clothes the last time you saw him?'

'I did not notice, sir. It is no concern of mine how folks dress.' Symes drew himself up; his tone became defensive, bordered on aggression. 'And if he bought them with the spoils of his trickery there is no way of proving it.'

'Such clothes are beyond the cleverest coney-catcher in Warwickshire. Nay, England, even.'

'A man dresses as becomes his trade, sir.'

'Exactly. To the peril of the gullible and the unwary. May the gentry, wherever his travels have taken him, beware his dress and his silver tongue lest they mistake him for one of their own and succumb to his wiles. His evidence was damning at the trial, and it went unquestioned.'

'He merely told what he saw, sir.'

'It flowed smooth enough from his tongue, truth or lie. Perhaps he was rewarded for his fine oration, constable?'

'Indeed not, sir!' The officer flushed with indignation. 'The Witchfinder has never been known to reward the truth, only to punish those who lie.'

'True enough.'

'I must about my business, sir, if you will excuse me. Edward Las, the highwayman, has robbed two of the justices of the peace on their return journey to Warwick. My men have ridden to try to arrest him and I have extra work to do in their absence.'

'I am sure that the ale will pass your discerning test in this fearsome heat, constable. I will delay you no longer from your duties.'

Guy Kent stood and watched Symes stride away. The other's ire was easily pricked. It was good sport in an idle moment. And sometimes it was necessary to stir muddy waters in an attempt to discover what lay beneath the surface.

Kent wondered if it was worth checking the cave and its surrounding area at Guy's Cliff again. The constabulary was not renowned for its thoroughness in searching. The place held a nostalgic lure for him and it would be cooler up there on the wooded hillside.

Also, he needed a place in which to smoke a secretive, meditative pipe of tobacco, and to dwell upon the mystery of Nicholas the coney-catcher's recently acquired expensive style of dress.

There was much he needed to mull over in his sharp, inquisitive mind.

William came from a long line of gamekeepers and the sad fact was that he would be the last of them because his wife was barren. Tall and muscular, his shoulders had begun to stoop a little at the approach of his fortieth year, a condition that was also partly due to the numerous occasions on which he had carried a shot stag home on his back.

His huge black beard was greying now, and beneath his soft velvet hunting cap his head was balding. He was rarely seen hatless; it was rumoured that he even slept in it. Perhaps the hair on his crown was starved of daylight and air, and had withered and died.

A tunic of dark green flecked with brown provided a camouflage against the vegetation in all seasons, and his heavy slops were tucked into knee-length soft cowhide boots; his step was stealthy at all times. A devotee of the crossbow, he scorned the scattershot matchlock which rusted in his outhouse. Guns were noisy; deer and poachers heard the report for miles around, and one never had the opportunity for a second shot, or a gang of poachers would flee leaving behind a minion with shattered legs.

The Ogre of the Forest, such was his reputation in the woods between Stratford and Warwick. His boundaries were far reaching and the Lord Lieutenant had bestowed upon him an authority equal to that of a constable. None liked him, most feared him, he shunned the alehouses knowing that familiarity bred contempt and that whilst he drank the poachers would ply their illegal trade.

Few saw him but he saw many, whether it was a legitimate

traveller passing beneath the thick bough upon which William lay at fell stretch or a hungry peasant, armed with a crude bow, in futile search of a beast to ward off starvation. A man of few words because he spoke to none except those who transgressed in his domain, the secrets of the forests were withheld from even his long-suffering wife.

Occasionally, he spied upon illicit lovers in a secluded dell, and his bearded lips would twitch in silent mirth. Yon wench's belly will be full ere long, he would muse, and then sadness would creep into his grey eyes as his thoughts turned to that which could never be his.

For he was the last of the true woodsmen. There were none fit to follow him.

In the summer months part of his duties to the manorial estate was to fell trees and cut logs. He liked this least of all for it was an irksome labour, preferring to be abroad on a moonlit night in search of poachers, or spying out the movements of the deer herds in readiness for when Richard ap Cynon decided to hunt.

William's life was one of freedom. He was bound by no fixed hours although he worked longer than a labourer in the fields. None monitored his movements; he was judged on results and often rewarded handsomely by the hunters if they had killed well.

He knew every path through those miles of deep forest as well as a townsman might know his neighbouring streets. Which was why he knew the whereabouts of Edward Las, the highwayman. The latter was currently inhabiting a cave in a small cliff face where the Welcombe Hills began, a remote setting which was only reached by following a twisting path trodden by the deer, and even then one was likely to become lost.

William marvelled that the other had ever found such a place of seclusion, for Las was no countryman. His habits were those of a city dweller; he did not know an oak from a beech, nor a rabbit from a hare. There was no fear of the fellow killing game for his larder for, marksman that he was reputed to be, his ignorance of woodcraft would not permit him to approach within pistol range of his intended quarry. Likewise, he was oblivious of the use of snares and he had no traps.

The constables rode the forest paths in search of their man but they had not passed within half a mile of his hideout. Nor would they, for they would only go where a horse could travel. They were too idle to go on foot, and no mount would negotiate that narrow and overgrown track.

William pondered upon the capture of Edward Las. A stealthy approach towards the cave entrance, a long wait until its inhabitant emerged, then a bolt shot straight and true. It would have been all too easy, but, on that occasion when Symes and the churchwarden had called at William's cottage to ask if he had perchance seen the villain, they had stated that they wanted Las alive. The public hanging of a notorious highwayman would enhance their reputation as upholders of the law, a corpse with a bolt through its heart would receive little publicity. Particularly if the shot had not been fired by either of themselves. A woodsman was no charismatic figure, and the incident would soon be forgotten.

William contemplated the possibility of taking the highwayman alive. The keeper was of huge stature, the robber was a weakling from the starving back streets of the city. In theory it would be no contest, in practice there was an unknown element of cunning attached to the other. Las had outwitted armed constables, had killed more than once. It was too great a risk.

So William decided upon a safe compromise. A *mantrap*.

The gamekeeper kept several mantraps set throughout the hours of darkness, mostly on little known tracks leading to places the deer were known to frequent, on the off chance of poachers attempting a nocturnal stalk.

Occasionally, on inspecting his traps, so that they might be sprung and rendered harmless to gatherers of kindling and beechmast by day, William came upon an imprisoned poacher. The fellow's legs were invariably mangled by the cruel sharp teeth, and twice Rhys, the physician, had had to carry out an amputation. One of the rascals had died before they were able to bring him to trial; several had hanged. What matter the mutilation of a man's legs if he was shortly to die?

So, that night, having reconnoitred by a secretive stalk to the cave entrance where William heard the steady breathing of a sleeping man, he retreated to the place where he had dragged his cruel engine of mutilation.

Mayhap he could have taken Las as he slept, overpowered him and bound him securely whilst Symes and his constables were summoned. But once the officers had their man, it would be all too easy to ignore him who had effected the capture. And there was a handsome reward. William had forgotten the amount offered, but in all likelihood not only would the credit be stolen by Symes or Martyn Wylde, but the parish coffers would be that much richer by nonpayment of the bounty. A trap was the only solution – they could scarcely deny that it had been set by the Lord Lieutenant's gamekeeper.

With practised ease and no small amount of strength, William dragged the trap across the narrow path and held down the jaws whilst he set it firm enough to resist the passage of a small creature of the forest, but so precisely that an unsuspecting man would have no chance to jump back before the iron teeth closed. Once caught, there was no escape.

William spread a light covering of last winter's dead oak leaves to hide the plate, stood back to admire the invisibility of his handiwork in the wan starlight. Even he must approach with care next morning in case he accidentally blundered into it! He shuddered at the prospect, pushed it from his mind.

Tonight he would sleep even sounder than usual in anticipation of his dawn trap inspection.

It was the departure of the gypsies which delayed the gamekeeper at daybreak next morning.

They were a damnable nuisance, always had been, no better than the vagrants that hung round the outskirts of Stratford. Worse, in fact, for vagrants did not inhabit the forest nor set snares for rabbits and hares. But for some reason Richard ap Cynon tolerated the Romanies' comings and goings so long as they did not poach the deer.

William left his cottage just as the eastern sky was paling grey and he had not gone a hundred yards before he heard the pitiful squealing of a coney caught in a noose. His long stride changed direction, and he was not surprised to come upon Cornelius carrying a rabbit, its legs still twitching, as if the fellow had every right to take it.

'You'm poaching rabbits agin, gypsy!' William's expression was hostile, his deep voice threatening.

'Catchin', not poachin', keeper, and well you know it!' The other stood his ground, defiant.

William hesitated, for Cornelius spoke the truth. Rabbits and hares were not denied to the wandering tribes, for truly the creatures did much harm to growing crops in the surrounding fields.

The keeper grunted. 'I thought you were moving on.'

'Within the hour. We should ha' gone yesterday, but Raol was not well. It was unwise to travel. She had a bout of exhaustion but she is fine now.'

William followed Cornelius back to where the single caravan was still parked, watched from a distance as the swarthy man skinned the rabbit, slow roasted it over a small fire. And breakfasted leisurely.

It was well over an hour before those wheels began to roll, and by then it was full daylight. William watched to make sure Cornelius and his woman headed towards the road, sighed his relief when they veered right at the rutted fork that would take them directly en route for Banbury. The woodsman had long learned not to take anybody's word for anything.

He turned back, picked up the trail that led off into the deep woods. Way ahead of him he heard jays screeching and magpies chattering, and knew that his trap was sprung. He hastened his step. Now the crows were calling, too. The scavengers of the forest had come to mock Man, their deadliest foe, perhaps even alight to peck at helpless flesh if the victim had lapsed into unconsciousness. Their favourite morsel was an eye, a corvid delicacy. William smiled to himself at the thought. Edward Lea would terrorise the highways no more.

The trap had done its work for sure. Even before he rounded the bend where it was set, a flock of crows, together with their more colourful relatives, flapped up into the air, screeching their protest at this unwarranted disturbance of their breakfasting.

In his mind, William saw the highwayman, bloodied legs bent and smashed, splinters of bone protruding from the lacerated flesh, lying backwards at an awkward angle, long having given up his feeble attempts to part the closed teeth. Unconscious, without a doubt, or else the corvid predators would not have alighted from the overhead boughs.

As he rounded the bend, William stopped, stared aghast at the scene which greeted him. No oath escaped his lips for he was not a vocal man, just an expelling of breath, a hint of nausea, for he had never before viewed such terrible mutilation.

The mantrap had most certainly caught but in a manner which he had never before experienced. The victim's legs were uninjured, sprawled on the path; arms had not flailed.

For somehow the unsuspecting man must have stumbled as he approached the concealed device, fallen headlong into it so that the waiting jaws had snapped shut upon his unprotected neck.

It was a terrible injury that might only have been surpassed by the guillotine, introduced a few years previously into Scotland by the Earl of Morton who was himself beheaded by it. Tales of its grisly work had even filtered south to the woods of Warwickshire.

The unfortunate man lying there on that remote woodland path had undoubtedly been decapitated. Attached only by a few sinews, his head hung down from the snapped jaws like a dislodged wasps' nest. His clothing was saturated from the blood which had spouted from the severed main artery.

William looked no closer, backed away. Shamefully he vomited his breakfast before setting off at a fast pace to summon the constables.

CHAPTER FOURTEEN

'You stink of tobacco worse than you did when you came home late last night.' Diana Hawker threw back the bedclothes, allowed the early morning sun shafting through the single window to bathe her nakedness in its golden glow.

A brief display of provocation; she slid beyond the reach of her lover's arms, laughed her remonstration. 'Clean breath and we may well have continued where we left off last night, Guy. At least I can rest assured that, coming home late with stale breath, you had not been with another woman. Certainly not one of any status.'

He laughed. 'Tobacco nourishes the brain, and mine needs fortifying for I am sure that my eyes see things which my brain does not translate into simple explanations.'

'Such as?'

'A man of newly acquired wealth takes to inhabiting a dank cave whereas he undoubtedly has the means to reside at an inn, should he choose to do so. Why does he not? He has had visitors at his lowly abode, well-booted men who have doubtless brought him sustenance in order that he may remain hidden. From whom? Myself, because I wish to question him about his fine clothes?'

'Nicholas is hiding out at Guy's Cliff?'

'Most certainly, but he did not return to the cave at dark for some reason. Where has he gone? I must find out, for I think that he holds

100

the key to this whole unsavoury business.'

'I am going to gather wild garlic from the forest today.' She began to dress. 'It seems that most of the townspeople seek immunity from this outbreak of typhus. The garlic in the garden is mostly sold so I must plunder Nature's store. I wonder what Rhys is prescribing? He is most likely sending his patients to the barber for blood-letting, possibly using leeches.' She grimaced at the thought.

'Take care.' There was concern on his boyish features. 'The forest is no safe place these days. Not that I fear Nicholas, for he will hide and skulk, but Las, the highwayman, is hiding out somewhere according to Constable Symes.'

'I'll be watchful.' She noticed that he strapped his pistol to his waist. 'Likewise yourself, even though your tobacco fumes will doubtless keep most at bay!'

'I am returning to town.' He drew her to him, kissed her soft lips and this time she did not resist. 'I can but watch and wait; at the moment all my leads seem to have petered out. I think that I shall keep an eye on Bill Symes. He is a sly fellow – I do not trust him. He seems a little too concerned lest I should speak with the coney-catcher. . .'

It was cool in the shade of the trees. Diana did not hurry for a quantity of garlic could be uprooted in a remarkably short time if one knew where to look for it. She would return only when her basket was full.

The atmosphere smelled rich, almost heady, scented with honeysuckle and wild willow herb, marred only by the occasional whiff of stinkhorn. She breathed deeply. It was good to be away from the cottage, even. One took one's own surroundings for granted, but she was grateful that she was not compelled to live within the town itself. Guy said that the stench of death there was unmistakable if you recognised it for what it was. Dead bodies were mounting up in the charnel house.

She found a patch of garlic, dug down into the peaty forest floor with the sharpened piece of iron she used for that purpose, unearthed a cluster of tubers and shook the clinging soil from them. There was a goodly bed of the herb here; it would take only a short time to fill her basket, enough to last for a few days.

It was a time to think of pleasant things, mostly of Guy. Perhaps she was being unfair to him, selfish, because she was afraid of marriage? No, for the relationship they had was no different from marriage except for the vows and neither of them needed those. It was the precariousness of his status that concerned her every time he was away from home. A spy, for that was what he was, an outcast from nobility as well as the poor. A man not to be trusted because he ran with the hare as well as the hunters, protected by his employers so long as he was useful to them.

And when that usefulness expired. . . That was what worried her, that and the fact that one day he might not return to the cottage. Mingling with criminals was a dangerous occupation; written authority from the Lord Lieutenant himself was no armoured breastplate to deflect a pistol ball or to buckle the blade of a dagger. Widowhood was a terrifying prospect in name, yet grieving for a slain lover was no different. One day she would marry Guy Kent.

One day. . .

She started, paused in her digging to listen. A faint drumming came from afar which she recognised as hoofbeats. The sound grew louder by the second, a mount that was being urged to even greater efforts by the moment. A rider in a hurry that boded a desperate mission.

Diana grabbed up her basket, remembered something that Guy had said about a highwayman being at large in the forest. Could this be he, a ruthless man fleeing from the law, one who might seize a woman to hold as hostage against the constables?

The ground vibrated, the approaching horseman was but a bend away. Diana glanced around. A spreading elder bush stood less than a couple of yards from her. She sprang for it, parted the spreading lower branches and stepped beneath them, allowed them to spring back into place. Her heart was pounding in time with the drumming hooves. Even now the horseman was rounding the bend, she had made it into hiding with only seconds to spare.

Cautiously, she parted the curtain of leaves, peered out. A jet black mare foamed with the sweat of its efforts. The rider was hunched forward, his long dark cloak billowing; his wide-brimmed hat was pulled hard down on his head, obscuring part of his face. But that which was still visible to the watching Diana was enough to recognise him by in spite of his contorted expression of fear. She gasped her surprise aloud.

The galloping horseman, stricken by unmistakable terror, was none other than Matthew King, the parish clerk.

Then he was hidden from view by the overhanging chestnut

branches, only a cloud of dust from the forest road and the fading sound of hooves evidence that Diana had not dreamed his passing.

She emerged from her hiding place, shook her head in puzzlement. From the direction in which King was heading, it would seem that he rode the forest road, the dangerous short cut, to Warwick. Possibly he had business there in his capacity as parish clerk but it was strange that he travelled at such speed on a surface that was rutted and holed; one false step by his steed could throw him, and his injuries would doubtless be severe. His expression was frightening to behold, that of a man who might have been pursued by Lucifer himself. An emergency, some kind of crisis, the possibilities were too numerous to contemplate. And, anyway, it was none of her business. All the same, she would mention it to Guy when he returned home tonight.

She continued with her task but her sense of peace and tranquillity was gone, leaving her with a feeling of tension that had her pausing to listen every so often.

Her basket was almost full of garlic cloves when she heard the unmistakable sound of a shot. It came from afar, muffled by the dense woodland, seemed to hang in the still air for some time. And when it was gone, she heard the birds of the woods shrieking their protests at this disturbance by Man. In the thickets jays and magpies screeched and chattered, their calling taken up by others in a cacophonic warning that danger was afoot.

Diana might have departed then, hastened homeward, except for the consoling thought that the shot had, in all probability, been fired by William, the gamekeeper. His duties demanded that he carried a weapon, either to take a deer for the manorial table or to kill rabbits that were ravaging the turnip crops. Maybe today he had chosen to carry his flintlock in preference to his customary crossbow.

She finished gathering her harvest and, for once, she was not sorry to leave the forest behind her.

A commotion outside the town hall attracted Kent's attention. Seldom did he partake of cider during the day but the bench outside the ale house seemed as good a vantage point as any without drawing undue attention to himself. Likewise, he could smoke without incurring the displeasure of others, for the company of aged peasantry were not concerned with the obnoxious habits of their fellows.

At first he was under the impression that a disturbance had broken out although it was early in the day for a brawl. Or perhaps somebody had died unexpectedly – an accident, possibly. Yet death rarely caused excitement, particularly in the midst of a typhus epidemic. Twice, during his vigil, the charnel wagon had rumbled past, a swarm of black flies in its wake.

A raised voice had brought the constables. A burly man, whom Kent recognised as the gamekeeper, was gesticulating wildly. Then Symes appeared, his dog bristling at his heels, barking at the gathering until the constable yelled at him to be quiet. One of the deputies was despatched upon an errand, left at a shambling run whilst the others grouped and waited. A crowd began to gather; Symes yelled at them to keep clear.

Two of the officers fetched horses from the stables, saddled and ready to ride. Everybody was looking down the street, impatiently waiting for somebody to join them.

Eventually the churchwarden appeared, his swift walk denoting urgency. The officers were bunched. Kent could just make out William's green hunting cap, the gamekeeper seemed to be the focus of attention.

Then they were climbing on to their horses, William an ungainly figure in the lead, alongside Martyn Wylde, as they cantered down the street. Folks emerged from dwellings and ale houses, stared after them. Something of a serious nature had occurred, possibly in the forest for the horsemen were heading that way, but none guessed the nature of the incident. Whatever, it must be serious for the churchwarden to ride with them.

Only then did Kent move. He hastened to the stable and demanded that the ostler make ready his horse, and a threepenny piece for the man if he hurried.

'There's sommat 'appened in the woods by the way they're riding.' The ostler craned his neck down the street but the dust kicked up by the horses hid the riders.

Guy Kent thrust a coin into the open palm, swung himself up into the saddle. He must not lose sight of the others, for the forest trails were numerous and the rock-hard ground was not conducive to tracking.

He kept the dust cloud in sight, saw where those ahead left the highway and turned into the forest. Kent eased his mount down to a canter, for at this stage he had no wish to catch up with those he followed.

The pounding of hooves and shouts reached him in the still air, so that he had no difficulty in determining which route they had taken at the fork. And then, without warning, on rounding a bend, he came upon the clustered group and was forced to haul on his reins. The sight of the mutilated corpse brought bile to his throat. The neck had finally severed and the head lay face downwards in the grass, sinews trailing like scarlet vipers. The body was slumped over the trap, a scarecrow in a field that had slipped from its support.

The others had dismounted, turned in surprise at the approach of a newcomer. Wylde's lips tightened; he made no show of concealing his irritation at the unwelcome arrival of Guy Kent. Symes grunted his own annoyance.

'What brings you here, Kent?' The churchwarden's tone was brusque; only the nagging reminder that the other carried manorial authority prevented him from voicing his disapproval further.

'I thought I would discover what all the excitement was about.' Kent swung himself down, smiled disarmingly. 'Surely there is no objection to my interrogating the dead man, churchwarden? Or have you already done that?'

'This is no time for jesting, Kent. A dangerous highwayman has been hiding out in these woods for weeks, has already robbed two justices of the peace from Warwick. I'll wager Richard ap Cynon will not be too displeased at the villain's untimely end.'

'Trapped like a wild animal.' Kent walked past the others, surveyed the bloodied body. 'A fate worse than the gallows.'

'But as good as my lord of Morton's guillotine.'

'How came it that he was trapped by his neck?'

Symes's eyes narrowed. This jackanapes was always questioning the obvious, looked for problems when there were none. 'He stumbled and fell, how else?'

'Over what, constable?'

The officer scanned the ground on both sides of the mantrap, swept it with a booted foot. There were neither stones nor protruding tree roots for an unwary walker to catch with his foot. 'Clumsiness. Maybe he fell over his own feet.'

'And he is the most desperately unlucky man in England, nay, the world, that where he falls there is a trap waiting, so precisely set that it beheads him!'

Glances were exchanged but none spoke. Kent moved across towards the severed head.

'Few will mourn the loss of Edward Las, highwayman and

105

murderer.' Bill Symes sniggered. 'Not even the most pious will shed a tear.'

'You speak for the people, constable,' Wylde added. 'But there are those who will be disappointed because yet another rogue has cheated the gallows.'

'And there's a reward,' the gamekeeper moved close to his trap. 'It was the trapper who caught the highwayman, deliberately. And expertly.'

'At the moment.' The churchwarden answered quickly, 'parochial funds are in some disarray. Doubtless the matter will be considered at a later date. Some small remuneration may well be made for your efforts, keeper. For the moment let us all be thankful that people can travel without the threat of being waylaid by a ruthless murderer.'

Kent rose from the scene of the decapitation, took a deep breath. His sunburn had paled, and there was a look of incredulity on his face. 'I beg to differ with you, churchwarden.'

'And what poppycock now?' The churchwarden's hands were on his hips, there was arrogance in his stance. Not even the Lord Lieutenant's stooge could disagree over a beheaded rogue.

'My deepest regret, gentlemen,' Kent's eyes swept the group, he addressed them all, 'is that I am no longer able to question Nicholas the coney-catcher on how he came by the means to purchase gentlemen's clothing.'

'You talk in riddles, Kent.' Wylde's hands clenched until his knuckles whitened. 'Enough of this play-acting, this time-wasting. Methinks you delay us for a reason, although I am at a loss to understand it. Pray move aside so that we can identify the corpse.'

'Most certainly.' Kent stepped to one side. 'It is a waste that fine clothing, newly purchased, should be ruined so soon.'

The churchwarden rolled the head with his boot, jumped back as if its teeth had bared, snapped at him: 'What trickery is this, Kent? Have you followed us deliberately to mock us because you knew from the outset what we should find here?'

'I had no idea why you rode out of town.' Guy Kent's expression was solemn. *'Indeed, it is as big a shock to myself to discover that it is not Edward Las who lies beheaded before us but, instead, the body of the man I have been diligently seeking. . . Nicholas, the coney-catcher.'*

CHAPTER FIFTEEN

Kent had remained at the scene of barbaric death after the churchwarden and his constables had departed. The gamekeeper had been ordered to bury the body where it lay for none would be interested in the untimely end of a trickster. Also, the charnel house was piling up with corpses awaiting interment; the gravediggers were overworked. There was no parson at the moment, either, so nobody was going to make a fuss over a corpse buried in unconsecrated ground, particularly in the midst of an outbreak of typhus. The priority was to bury the dead to prevent the spread of disease.

Wylde had hinted at the possibility of some 'small remuneration' for William's efforts, perhaps to alleviate the woodsman's disappointment at discovering that he had trapped a rascal and not a wanted highwayman, and thus was not eligible for a reward.

'Go and fetch your shovel, keeper, whilst I make a few observations of the corpse and its surroundings.' Kent waited until the sound of hoofbeats had faded before he moved, stooped and parted the grasses in order to see the ground beneath the stalks.

'The ground is baked hard by the drought. Footmarks will not show.' William watched the other, understood the thinking of a tracker for it was second nature to himself. 'The grass might have been trodden flat but it will have sprung back up by now. Except where those oafs have trampled it like milling oxen.'

'Alas, you are right.' Kent made no attempt to hide his disappointment. 'And, as the constable so smugly confirmed, there are neither stones nor roots to trip the unfortunate fellow.'

"Tis right enough.'

'The chances of a man falling head first into a trap are too remote even to consider.' Kent stroked his chin meditatively. 'Would not you say so, keeper?'

'They put him in the trap, either dead or alive, it makes no difference.' William's bearded expression was grim. He glanced about him, perhaps fearing that somebody lurked in the nearby bushes, listening.

'*They?*'

'Somebody, I have no idea who, I swear it.' A sudden fear that he might have left himself open to accusation. ' A strong man might do it on his own.' Guilt because he himself was big and strong.

'You are right, but we can prove nothing because there are no marks on head or body except those left by the teeth of the trap. The most important man in this dark mystery, I believe, was Nicholas. Now he has been murdered because it was known that I wished to question him about how he came by the money to buy his fine clothes. He had aroused my suspicions; it was better for somebody if he was dead.'

'And now you will never know the answers to the questions you wished to ask.' William eyed his companion suspiciously. The gamekeeper trusted none.

'Certainly not from the coney-catcher, but there are others.' Kent had the feeling that whoever had perpetrated the recent foul deeds was becoming desperate, running scared. From himself. And that made him uneasy enough to subconsciously check that the pistol was still in his belt.

'I'll fetch my shovel. . .'

The gamekeeper was interrupted by the sound of a shot. It froze both men momentarily. The report was muffled by the forest but it could not have been more than a few hundred yards away from where they stood.

'A shot, keeper. Poachers?'

'No poacher uses a pistol, particularly by day, and that was neither scattergun nor rifle. The only pistol I know in these woods belongs to Edward Las.'

'Come, let's tread stealthily.' Kent turned, catlike, and headed down a winding path that led in the direction from which the shot had come. Suddenly events were moving fast. Too fast.

William hesitated. He had no wish to be confronted by the notorious highwayman. Perhaps the villain knew that an attempt had been made to trap him, and had used Nicholas as bait in order to draw his hunters into a trap of his own. Yet the gamekeeper could not be seen to be a coward by his companion. Reluctantly, he followed at the other's heels, keeping a safe distance in case an ambush was planned.

It was as though every jay and magpie in the forest was calling, rejoicing over a human death. Possibly it was a premonition of another. Kent pushed the thought from his mind. He needed to be alert in every sense.

He looked behind him, deliberately slowed to allow the other to catch up. The gamekeeper was a scared man, and often it was better to be alone than to have a frightened companion. Then his nostrils flared. He sniffed the air, smelled an aroma that was familiar to him yet out of place in these woodlands. 'I smell powdersmoke. We are close.'

The other nodded. He, too, had scented a whiff of burned saltpetre, the main ingredient of coarse gunpowder. On a still day it was reluctant to disperse. Whoever had fired that shot up ahead should have used a crossbow, which was both silent and odourless. And deadly.

Silence. Not even the birds were calling now; it was as though they huddled fearfully on the boughs, watched and waited in anticipation of another human death.

Kent slid the pistol out of his belt, eased the hammer back carefully so that it did not click. If anything moved in the foliage, he would fire. Both their lives were at risk.

He moved forward, walked on the balls of his feet, brushed the grass with his sole before lowering his weight in case he cracked a dead twig. The foliage on both sides of the track was dense, could have hidden a hundred highwaymen.

The stench of pistol smoke was heavy and rancid, and he fought off the urge to cough. They were close, very close. Perhaps round the next bend. . .

Something moved up ahead, just out of sight. Kent's pistol came up in readiness, was trained unwaveringly on the bend in the path, his forefinger resting on the trigger ready to apply a full pressure.

A horse neighed, shifted impatiently. Kent dropped into a crouching position, took the bend at a run. Then he pulled up, aghast for the second time within the hour at the scene which greeted him.

The horse shied at his sudden appearance, kicked its hind legs and bolted. The saddle was empty.

Because its rider lay huddled in the middle of the small clearing and one glance was sufficient for Kent to know that the other was dead.

The inert man's cloak was spread like a hastily arranged black shroud in a vain attempt to hide the bloodied features from whoever might chance upon this scene of violent death. A wide-brimmed hat lay a few yards away. And gripped in the motionless fingers of the outstretched arm was a pistol, smoke still wisping up from its muzzle.

Kent was still cautious, turned a full circle, his weapon at the ready. William emerged from the track they had followed, started at what he saw. The dead man's forehead was shattered, a gaping wound from which blood gushed, the mouth wide in what might have been a death scream that had never materialised.

'He took his own life. Or perhaps it was an accident due to an unfamiliarity with firearms.' The gamekeeper hesitated to pre-judge; it was often dangerous to voice one's personal opinions. You never knew who might be listening.

Kent's eyes narrowed. Recognition was not easy – the features were awash with scarlet – yet the profile, the clothing, were only too familiar.

'*Matthew King, the parish clerk!* ' William confirmed his companion's suspicions.

'And dead, his brains blown out, the smoking pistol in his own hand.' Guy Kent spoke aloud, recalled the churchwarden's recent remark about the parochial funds being in disarray. It probably meant nothing. 'Keep your distance, keeper. Let me see if by any chance *this* dried ground tells me anything.'

It didn't, not so much as a hoofmark. Kent turned his attention to the dead man. Accident or suicide, there was something that was not quite right. 'Keeper, a man has just blown his brains out, whether by mistake or intent is immaterial. Do you notice anything?'

William's forehead furrowed the way it always did when he concentrated. He was not a thinking man – he relied upon his eyes and his instincts. But he knew from experience how an animal discovered dead in the forest had died, could tell by the wound at what range it had been shot with ball or bolt.

"Tis strange, sir,' he whispered, for he was not accustomed to being asked for his opinion, 'but if the gentleman turned the barrel on himself, the flesh would have been burned by the powder flash. Likewise, the wound would have been bigger.'

'Exactly! This man has been shot close but not within the reach of his own arm!' Kent looked about him. The horse stood at a distance watching them. He noted how some fronds of bracken on both sides of the path had been snapped, fresh sap oozing from the breaks. Stout ash trees grew behind the foliage. He walked across, took care where he trod.

Kent's expression was one of satisfaction. A hunch, albeit a small

110

one, had proved its worth. He peered round the other side of the trunk just to make sure. The bark was scored in a ring that ran right round the tree without a break. Sap oozed out of the abrasion.

'Hmm!' Kent checked the tree immediately opposite on the other side of the track; it was marked in exactly the same way.

'A tethered horse, perhaps two.' The gamekeeper was following his companion's train of thinking.

'No,' Kent pointed to the bracken. 'A horse would have trampled it flat. A man trod it down when he tied a rope around both trees, stretched it across the path at just the right height to dislodge a passing horseman!'

'The rider was knocked from his mount and then. . .'

'Shot, but unfortunately not close enough to make suicide plausible. The pistol was then placed in King's hand and the killer departed, satisfied that he had fooled whoever might find the body. Clever, but not clever enough.'

'Las?'

'A possibility.'

'Why would he go to all that trouble? Why not just rob him, shoot him if he had to?'

'There was no robbery. See, the murdered man still wears his money pouch.' Kent knelt, shook the pouch, heard it jangle. 'Robbery was not the motive but I think for the moment, keeper, both you and I will pretend to believe that King took his own life.'

'As you wish, sir.' Suspicion clouded the gamekeeper's keen eyes. He was neither a devious nor a dishonest man.

'Thank you. Now, please continue with the burial of Nicholas. In the meantime, I shall ride to Stratford and inform the churchwarden and the constable.'

'I will do as you request, sir.'

'As the churchwarden requested, William.' Guy Kent smiled as he corrected him. 'Oh, and just one other thing that puzzles me. Why would the parish clerk, whether he was murdered or took his own life, be riding along a remote woodland track?'

'He might have been going to Warwick, sir. It is the quickest way if you have no regard for footpads and highwaymen. Which might have been why he rode armed. Do you not think, sir,' William always looked for the simplest explanation to all problems, 'that King might have been confronted by Las after having been knocked from his horse, and been shot when he drew his pistol?'

'No.' Kent led the way back to where his horse waited patiently.

'There was only one shot, keeper, and the pistol that fired it was clutched in Matthew King's hand when we found him.'

Martyn Wylde was in the room which he used as an office in the town hall, the door partly ajar. Kent saw as he approached it that the churchwarden had company, Constable Symes and a deputy. There appeared to be an atmosphere of frenetic activity: documents had spilled on to the floor, calf-bound ledgers were open, some of them propped on chairs.

'Here is the warrant.' The churchwarden scratched on it with a quill, waved it to dry the ink on his scrawled signature. 'Saddle your horse, constable, and go after him straightway. Bring him back under arrest!'

'I will do my best, sir, although there is no knowing which way he has gone.'

'Ask any of those drunken idlers who spend their day drinking outside the ale houses. Somebody is sure to have seen Matthew King leaving town. He is hardly inconspicuous.'

'I'll leave at once, churchwarden. I will take a couple of constables with me so that we can cover more ground. I—'

'I think I can save you the trouble, constable.' Kent appeared in the doorway, did not fail to notice the hostile glances cast in his direction.

'Kent!' Martyn Wylde was visibly controlling his anger. 'Please do not delay Constable Symes; his mission is of the utmost urgency.'

'No longer.' Kent smiled affably, stepped inside the room. 'Forgive me, I did not mean to eavesdrop but I could not help overhearing your conversation. At this very moment Matthew King lies dead upon the forest route to Warwick!'

'Unbelievable!' Both Wylde and Symes had blanched. 'A victim of the highwayman, doubtless, perhaps revenge for our setting a trap for him. Or possibly a common hold-up, for the parish clerk is known to carry revenue from taxes collected.'

'Suicide, I believe,' Kent murmured. 'I cannot be absolutely sure, for I gave the body no more than a cursory glance, but King's pistol was clutched in his hand and it had been fired recently. As a matter of fact, the gamekeeper and I heard the shot from where we stood by the trickster's body.'

'We also heard a shot as we rode back.' Wylde glanced at Symes. 'We thought it was perhaps the gamekeeper so we did not turn back.'

'It is strange that the parish clerk should take his own life.' Kent wore a puzzled look. 'Stranger still that he chose to ride deep into the forest to do it. Surely, just inside the trees would have been adequate if he was in that frame of mind.'

'He had every reason to take his own life.' Wylde waved a deprecating hand in the direction of the strewn documents and ledgers: 'He fled because I had discovered his fraud, a gross misappropriation of parochial funds. Even now I am not sure of the amount but it is a small fortune stolen over a period of months. He knew that his theft had been unearthed, and fled blindly. Doubtless, he knew that he would be pursued, brought back to hang.' The churchwarden leaned forward; there was no mistaking his expression of anxiety. 'Kent, was he by any chance carrying bags of money?'

'A pouch containing a few groats. I did not trouble to count them.'

'Let us hope that the money is hidden somewhere and that we shall yet find it.' The other wrung his bony hands together in a gesture of anguish. 'Just as I pray to God that we shall locate the artefacts stolen from the church by the monk and his moonmen accomplices. I fear that the wrath of Richard ap Cynon will descend upon every parish official for not preventing these crimes.'

Symes shuffled his booted feet, stared down at them. For sure the blame would be apportioned to the constabulary; it always was. The churchwarden was a hard taskmaster.

'Two violent deaths within the hour!' Kent pursed his lips.

'And many more dying from typhus.' Wylde stretched his thin lips. 'It seems, though, that the gallows are destined to remain idle. Still, we cannot remain here bemoaning our ill fortune. Symes, send a deputation to bring in the parish clerk's body. Much as I would like to bury the scoundrel in the forest and have done with him, I fear that the bishop would protest to the Lord Lieutenant.' He tore the warrant, shredded it and let the fragments shower over the floor. 'Kent, I feel that the death of a beggar, which seems to trouble you most, is somewhat irrelevant in the midst of our crises.'

'Perhaps,' the other moved towards the door, 'perhaps not. Good day to you, churchwarden. I will not hinder you further for I can see that you are more than busy. I will content myself with some of the Swan's excellent fare and leave you to your business.'

The charnel wagon rumbled its way down Chapel Street followed by a swarm of black flies. The hessian sacking was piled high; it was a full load.

113

Death, it seemed, was an hourly occurrence these days.

CHAPTER SIXTEEN

'You *saw* him!' Guy Kent stared across the table in disbelief. 'You mean you actually saw Matthew King in the forest shortly before he died?'

Diana Hawker paused in the act of sorting garlic cloves into a wooden bowl. 'Yes, and then I heard a shot some distance away. I presumed it was either the gamekeeper or some poachers. In either case, it was no business of mine.'

'You were in deadly danger.' The beads of sweet which glinted on Kent's brow had nothing whatsoever to do with the sultry heat of early evening. 'A desperate killer was lurking within yards of where you gathered garlic. He probably watched you.'

'Are you sure that the parish clerk did not take his own life, Guy?'

'Positive. But the mystery deepens.'

'He was clearly upset or frightened, perhaps both. I feared lest his horse might collapse beneath him under the strain of being forced to keep up that pace in the sweltering heat.'

'The track he rode was a short cut to Warwick.' Kent became thoughtful. 'If Matthew King was fleeing from justice, or injustice, then Warwick was the most dangerous place in England for him. He would be known there, and even had the constables not been hard on his heels his presence would have been noted and it would have been that much easier to follow him. It puzzles me why he fled with such haste, for even on my return from the forest the churchwarden was only just issuing a warrant for his arrest. King had at least two hours' start on his pursuers. And why did he not head south to Banbury or Oxford, make his way to London where the teeming masses would swallow him up? And maybe even hide himself in the audience and watch one of the bard's plays.' He laughed softly.

'You are convinced that Edward Las killed Matthew King?'

'As certain as I can be. Just as I believe that the highwayman killed the coney-catcher by pushing him head first into a barbaric mantrap. But the key to the whole business, I feel, rests on *why* King was riding to Warwick. Alas, yet another who might have shed some light on this dark business has been silenced.'

'And Ned the Beggar? He seems to have been forgotten lately.'

'No, he was the start of this whole chain of murders. His death must not have been in vain.' There was a grim determination in his expression.

'What are you going to do now, Guy?' She cut a corm, popped it into her mouth. Garlic was an antidote for most ailments, including the unpleasantness of a tobacco smoking lover.

'Las could tell me a lot, I'll warrant.'

'Guy, *no!*'

'I'll wager he's no more dangerous than those who have used him. Certainly, he has not their brains, just animal cunning. He could have been caught by now – methinks there are those who do not want him arrested because he is too useful to them whilst he remains at large. I fear that before too long his body will be found somewhere, a ball between the eyes or a dagger in his back.'

'You are only guessing?'

'A feeling, but I've nothing to lose by pursuing it.'

'Except your life. They will kill you as cold-bloodedly as they have murdered the others.'

'They would like to.' Kent had never before appreciated the sheer beauty of a snaphance pistol. He fondled it almost lovingly, weighed its perfect balance in his hand. A nobleman's weapon made by a craftsman, the fishtail butt fitted snugly into his palm. He noted the *JL* engraved upon the lock with a flourish of pride by the maker, James Low of Dundee. 'But they might not find me so easy to kill as the others.'

He stood up, took a powder and shot flask from a drawer in the tall dresser. Tonight he might have need to reload; relying upon a single shot was too risky when one's life depended upon the outcome.

'Let us suppose that Matthew King was not fleeing for his life, that he was riding to Warwick for a very different reason. . .'

'Too many suppositions, I fear, Guy.'

'Yes.' He came behind her, slipped his arms around her and kissed her slender neck. 'They need to be substantiated, and that is what I have to do tonight.'

'Take care.' She had long ago abandoned all hope of dissuading him from embarking upon dangerous missions.

'I will.' He strode out of the open door to where his horse grazed the

115

scorched grass of the small orchard.

The sun was dipping behind the western horizon as Kent rode out of town. The wooded Welcombe Hills were shrouded in a faint mist that promised another fine day on the morrow. Not that he doubted that the weather would be anything else. When a change was imminent you would sense it in the atmosphere, a cool dampness, the far hills starkly outlined instead of hazy.

Tonight Kent scented danger, a feeling to which he responded, a kind of revitalisation, as though he had slumbered and was now fully awake. Every sense was alert. Even as he had ridden from the town he had scanned the faces of every watching bystander in case there was one he recognised who might be interested in his movements. But there were only blank stares and mild curiosity. A woman was weeping, probably a recent widow whose spouse had succumbed to the typhus outbreak. It made him think of Jane and how she had died needlessly.

The forest seemed to glower at him as if it sought to drive him away in case he discovered its terrible secret. Beneath the trees the shadows created night when outside it was still barely dusk; the stench of stinkhorn, the woodland fungus that attracts flies with its odour of putrefaction, was like a whiff from the charnel house far behind, a reminder of death. It had the adrenaline pumping in his veins. He responded to the challenge by kicking the flanks of the big black. It had been a long time since he had diced with death. Too long.

Once inside the forest he was forced to slow his pace, waiting whilst his eyesight adjusted to the gloom. It was far from easy riding along woodland tracks at night; one put one's trust in a faithful steed and ducked down to dodge low branches. In some ways Kent felt safer in the darkness, when he was no easy target for a waiting marksman. Unless, of course, a rope was stretched across the path ahead   of him. . .

He crouched even lower, hoped that he could retrace the winding track which he had ridden only that morning. Somewhere up ahead it forked; he must not miss the left hand parting of the ways. The highwayman had probably moved on; that was logical reasoning, not the thoughts of a coward seeking an easy way out. The horse moved easily, preferring the cool of the night to the heat of the day. It was an intelligent beast, too; at the first hint of another human being it would shy. Kent's fingers brushed the butt of his pistol, instinctively seeking reassurance. He was no mean marksman, he knew he was an even match for the man he hunted. Provided it was a fair duel in the open, naturally. Which was not Edward Las's way.

An orange glow filtered down through the leafy canopy. Praise be, there was a moon tonight and a full one at that! A mixed blessing, it enabled one to see in places in the deep forest but it also created shadows. Kent would need to rely upon his horse's keenness of scent and hearing more than ever, for moonlight favoured the ambusher.

He took the left fork, thought about dismounting. Not yet – when he came closer to his destination, perhaps. He could leave the animal untethered. It would not stray, which was as well for he might have need of it ere long.

He wondered again why Symes and his constabulary had not raided the highwayman's cave. Possibly William had not alerted them to the other's presence there, hoping that he might yet claim the offered reward. The constable was too dull to associate the setting of a trap in a particular place with the proximity of the scoundrel; the gamekeeper sets traps nightly, it was a speculative attempt. Kent became anxious for his horse, for a beast did not sense a steel trap until it was too late.

He glimpsed the moon. It had climbed quickly into the velvet sky, a huge orange ball that resembled a winter sun. His thoughts turned to witches and how legend had it that grotesque hags were able to bring down the moon by dancing naked and beating each other with birches; and how they supposedly flew through the sky on their brooms. Diana had a plausible theory, experienced as she was in the ways of herbs and brews: the crones drank belladonna and hallucinated, even believed their poisoned dreams themselves.

He found himself scanning the sky in search of a flying silhouette with a pointed hat and streaming cloak. He started, but the gasp had hardly escaped his lips before he recognised the outlines of arrowing mallards flighting to their nocturnal feeding place. His nerves were taut. It was too long since he had been on such a mission; two years, maybe three, since he had trailed the Brothers of Gaboriau to their afforested lair when—

The shot shattered the stillness of the summer night. The ball had cut through the crown of Kent's felted hat and whipped it from his head before he heard the report, saw the vivid flash from the other side of the clearing. Even then he might have stayed in the saddle had not his horse reared and whinnied in terror.

His instinct was to kick free of the stirrups in case the beast fell and rolled on him. He might have clutched at the reins or the mane, fought to get his mount back under control, but such an action would have presented him as an easy target should the ambusher have carried two pistols.

Kent released his grip, used the bucking saddle as a springboard, felt it catapult him into the air. He soared, reached the apex of his momentum, and only then did he draw up his legs and clasp his hands protectively to cover his head.

Somersaulting, a wave of vertigo hit him. He saw the moon, dazzling orange turning to bright yellow as it disappeared from his view. Now blackness that might have been a deep abyss falling down to Hades itself. A total loss of direction and distance – he had no idea how far he had to fall. His greatest fear was that he might strike an unyielding bole, snap his neck or back. He was at the mercy of his fate, and could do nothing to alter it.

For a brief moment he seemed to float, like that peasant protestor who had somehow dodged the guards and scaled the battlements of Warwick Castle a few years ago. Crowds had gathered in the street to watch, had seen the man leap into space, drop like a stone until his coat had billowed and checked his fall. But only momentarily; his remains had to be shovelled up in the courtyard, and rumour had it that they had been fed to the hunting hounds. But one could not always rely upon the authenticity of hearsay. Certainly, the unfortunate had broken every bone in his body.

Unlike that poor fellow, Guy Kent landed softly in a clump of bracken and thick grasses, so gently that it might have been the bed back at Diana's cottage on which he sprawled. It was almost luxurious, all the more so in the knowledge that he had survived his fall without apparent injury. He had cheated death with the first hand but there was a second to be played.

He lay there winded, his thoughts disoriented, a sense of relief which he knew he must dispel at once. Listening; a pounding of hooves that grew fainter with every passing second. The horse had bolted for home and who could blame it?

The echoes of the shot seemed to take an eternity to die away. Somewhere, not far away, an owl was hooting its protest at this disturbance; roosting birds were twittering uneasily in the dense foliage. Otherwise, there was only silence.

Kent lay perfectly still, his only movement to ease the snaphance out of his belt. He lay awkwardly on his back, staring up through tall fronds at the night sky. He dared not move, for his only chance was to feign unconsciousness or death.

A rolling of his eyes afforded him a partial view of the clearing, an area some twenty yards in diameter with levelled tree stumps jutting up out of the ground. Doubtless, William had felled the trees for logs and in so doing had created an arena for sudden death. A perfect place for an ambush: the open ground, flooded with ethereal moonlight, enabled the lurker to see without being seen; it gave him cover and protection from return fire, an opportunity to flit away when his foul deed was done.

And still there was silence. Had Edward Las, for surely it was he, departed, believing the man who trespassed in his domain to be dead?

No! Kent sensed the other before he heard him, another human presence that was revealed to him before he heard the rasping breath, a footfall that might have been stealthy in an unlit alleyway but was not so in a darkened forest. A movement that denoted the fear of a hunter looking for a shot wolf in cover and not knowing if it was truly dead.

Carefully, slowly, Kent eased back the hammer of his pistol and mentally thanked James Low for his craftsmanship in making a cocking device that operated with such smoothness and in silence. His grip tightened on the butt, the barrel lay flat along his canions. He waited, strained his eyeballs to their very limit. Would the other cross the clearing or would he make a detour and approach from the trees behind?

Mercifully, Edward Las, for undoubtedly it was he, chose to skirt the clearing. Possibly he feared that, not being skilled in woodcraft, his stalk would not go unheard. He took advantage of every shadow, as he would have done in the city, moving from patch to patch, his ungainly form shambling with menacing intent. Capped and cloaked, it was impossible to discern in the wan light if he wore the domino mask that added to his malevolent appearance rather than disguised his features. The true ogre of the forest. Even Kent's blood ran cold for a second. And then he became the functioning machine of efficiency and cool nerve that had earned him the post bestowed upon him by the Lord Lieutenant. Gone was his fear; there was a job to be done, and the very key which might unlock these vile secrets was within ten yards of where he lay.

Kent fired from the position he was in, for to have raised himself up might have alerted the other and given him the opportunity to spring away; there would be no time to reload.

Once again the forest reverberated to an explosive detonation, and the clearing was vividly lit. Kent saw his man straighten up, the broad back seeming to arch; the pistol exploded before it fell from the highwayman's grasp, the ball ploughing harmlessly into the ferny floor. And as Kent leaped to his feet he saw his adversary crumple, sink to the ground.

Kent had intended a shoulder shot, one that would have smashed bone yet not been fatal provided the wound was staunched quickly. One that would have rendered return fire impossible. A warning would only have served to alert such a man, resulted in either evasive action or retaliation. One who faces the gallows inevitably prefers to go down to a ball.

Las lay in a shaft of moonlight, his features contorted; he was not wearing his mask. Kent saw the blood starting to flow from the twisted lips, knew then that his own marksmanship had been at fault. A ground-level shot is never easy, and he had neglected to practise it lately. Half-light is deceptive; a sudden movement, perhaps a stumble, by the intended victim can make the difference between a shoulder and a chest shot. But excuses were worthless, simply a sop to his pride.

Edward Las had been shot in the chest. The ball had smashed his breast bone and severed a lung. The blood came faster, began to pump. His eyes were closed.

'Las, can you hear me?' Kent dropped to a knee, shook the other roughly. It would make no difference to the inevitable outcome.

Those eyes opened, reflected pain and fear. For Las the moment that every robber feared had arrived. He spoke, a gurgle of spouted claret. His powerful body shook. He had heard all right.

'Tell me quickly, man,' Kent's expression was merciless, 'you killed the coney-catcher, put his head in the jaws.' It was not a question, merely a statement requiring confirmation.

Another deluge of lung blood; the squat head nodded. Maybe it was a dying boast.

'And Matthew King, you fetched him from his horse with a rope, shot him with your pistol and placed it in his hand so that it would seem that he took his own life. I'll warrant that that is his pistol with which you tried to kill me.'

A definite affirmative nod that terminated in a spasm of coughing. The blood was coming faster now.

'Can you speak, man? Make an effort.'

A guttural sound, it might have been 'aye'. The highwayman's eyes closed.

'A last chance to purge your soul, Las, do just one good thing in your wasted life. *Tell me who paid you to kill the coney-catcher and the parish clerk. They cannot harm you now. It is they who killed you, not I. For doubtless they have paid you to kill me, too. A name – give me a name before it is too late!* '

The lips moved, struggled to speak. Another gush of blood. Kent bent his head, mentally urging the other. He heard a liquid wheezing within that shattered chest, the mouth spat crimson.

And in that instant Edward Las's head fell sideways and his body went limp. His last sound was an exhalation of wind.

CHAPTER SEVENTEEN

'A good night' s work, Kent,' Martyn Wylde smiled grudgingly, looked up from behind a table littered with documents and open ledgers, 'but I doubt whether your position will allow you to claim the reward offered for Edward Las. A pity, though, that you did not bring him in alive. It would have been fitting to hang such a notorious character in Stratford. I'd wager we would have drawn a bigger audience than does the Globe theatre in London!'

'I trust that the discrepancies in the taxes and tithes are not as bad as you at first thought?' Kent countered, saw how the other's lips tightened.

'Worse, I fear.' The churchwarden grimaced. 'I still do not have a final figure but when I do it will be a very large sum. Unless it is recovered I fear that there will be neither maintenance of the roads nor food for the poor in the next year. The fellow was clever. His figures have been falsified for months. It was only by chance that I perceived a minor discrepancy in the taxes collected and, on looking into it, discovered to my horror that other substantial amounts had been misappropriated. I must ride to Warwick today and inform the Lord Lieutenant. Unless, of course, the money can be recovered in time. At this very moment Symes and his men are searching Matthew King's house; all panelling is being removed in an endeavour to find a secret cache. I hope, too, that the church artefacts can be found ere long. Doubtless I shall be removed from my post, for the ultimate responsibility rests with myself.'

Kent felt a fleeting pity for the other. A hard man, disliked by many for the nature of his position, Wylde was likely to face trial for his negligence. Possibly Symes would be punished, too, for failing in his duties to locate the missing property.

'I will assist with the search,' Kent said. 'It seems to me that for some reason the cave at Guy's Cliff was favoured by villains.'

'Everybody dreams of coming upon the hidden trove.' The other smiled whimsically. 'It will be a lure for many years to come if it is not found. Just as the treasure in the Wash is still being searched for, it will draw villains from all over the country in the hope of untold riches. Doubtless that was why Edward Las took up residence in the forest. There will be others. Let us pray that it will be found. And speaking of prayer reminds me, our departed parson is being buried today. I must attend before I leave to take the ill tidings to Warwick. There are funerals daily; there is no sign of the plague checking. I fear that Rhys has done little to stem it and neither,' his lips stretched in an expression that embodied sarcasm, 'has your own fair lady in spite of her innumerable herbal remedies. Fortunately, most of the deaths are amongst the poor; let us hope that it remains so.'

'I shall keep my eyes and ears open in the hope of locating the missing treasure.' Kent turned on his heel and went back out into the street.

Right now it seemed that every possible clue had died along with those who might have been able to help him.

Diana had spent most of the afternoon attempting to remove the blood spotlets from Guy's green canions; his bright yellow socks were still soaking in a pail of water. Her efforts had frustrated her, and she almost lost faith in her own soap made from fats and scented with primrose oil. Her only consolation was that the stains were from the highwayman's blood and not her lover's; trunk hose and canions were easily renewed, Guy was irreplaceable.

Last night, tossing restlessly in bed, she had again argued the merits and shortcomings of marriage with herself. It was the waiting for him to return, fearing that he might not, that was the worst; the worry was the same whether Guy was husband or lover. She wished earnestly that Richard ap Cynon would transfer him to other, less dangerous, duties. But Guy did not want that. His challenge in life was taking on seemingly unsolvable mysteries and cunning villains. His job was not to hunt down dangerous highwayman, that was the constables' duty. Unless, of course, the chase had a bearing on the case.

Now she pegged the canions on a length of rope stretched between two stunted apple trees. The garments would dry stained; they would only be suitable to wear whilst doing gardening chores. Which Guy resisted until his every possible excuse had run out. She sighed; she loved him all the more for that. And suddenly marriage had a distinct appeal. All the same, she would not rush into it. She had resisted it for five years now, another few weeks would not make any difference. Except that she, too, was running out of excuses.

Guy returned home earlier than expected. For once he appeared morose, left his horse to graze the orchard grass.

'A drink of camomile brew will refresh you.' She reached a stone flagon from the cool of the small larder.

'It's welcome, but I do not think it will help other than to quench a raging thirst.' He sank down into the rocking chair, resisted the temptation to produce his pipe. 'A day of distinct non-events.' Briefly he related his conversation with the churchwarden. 'It would appear that Matthew King was stealing from parochial funds to no small degree.'

'Which accounts for the distressed state in which I saw him yesterday morning.'

'Yes, but why was he riding to Warwick? Why was Edward Las hired to kill him? The constables could have arrested King, he would have gone to the gallows. Surely, logically, that would have been a more fitting conclusion to the matter? Las confessed that he murdered him, made it look like suicide, but why? He did not even rob him. I fear there are even deeper and murkier waters beneath the surface scum which I have yet to stir. Oh, that Edward Las had held out for another few seconds, just long enough to utter a name.'

'But he didn't, he died.' She handed him a drinking vessel. 'And his secret died with him. Now you will never find out. Let matters rest, Guy, please.'

'No.' He took a long drink. 'I feel I am so close, yet so far. The rogues are convinced they have covered their tracks; all who could have told are dead. Now I must wait for the scoundrels to make a mistake. The church artefacts and the parish money are missing, well hidden. Some time they have to surface or else their acquisition is pointless.'

'They are probably on their way to London, possibly even there already, Guy.' It was futile trying to persuade him to give up but she tried all the same.

'I think not.'

'Why?'

'Just a feeling I have. Far better to let the hue and cry die down before transporting them. Wylde is riding today to try to make his peace with the Lord Lieutenant. He may escape with a reproach – he is silver-tongued enough. The constable will be the scapegoat.'

'For which I shall not shed a single tear.' She poured some camomile for herself. 'A sly fellow, not to be trusted. And that dog of his should be shot. It has savaged a number of innocent people.'

'All in the cause of upholding the law, I am afraid.' Guy rose to his feet. 'It's airless in here. Why sit indoors on a fine evening? I'm going to go and relax in the orchard.'

'I'll come with you.' She caught his expression, wagged a finger. 'Oh yes I am, to ensure that you don't smoke and foul your breath and pores before bed!'

'Tobacco repels the insects on a sultry night.'

'And so does this!' She reached a container of ointment from the dresser.

'Garlic!' He sniffed his disapproval. 'Our lives seem to revolve around the herb, whether to purify the blood or to ward off the plague. . .'

'And ward off the insects.' She began smearing some on her face. 'No herb does it better. Even the caterpillars shun my cabbages when I water the leaves with a garlic solution.'

It was pleasantly cool in the orchard once the sun had dropped behind the Welcombe Hills and dusk began to creep across the meadows. Reluctantly, Guy admitted that the clouds of midges kept their distance. Even so, he longed for a smoke of fragrant tobacco. If only Diana would go indoors to attend to some chore, he could sneak a pipe; the garlic would destroy the evidence.

'The moon will rise shortly.' she rested against him. 'I missed it last night, unfortunately.'

Which meant that she was not likely to retire for some time. He abandoned all hope of a smoke. Lately it had become almost a craving, in the way that the alehouse idlers were addicted to their

124

brew.

The sky began to lighten with a radiant orange glow and a few minutes later the tip of the moon peeped over the far tree-lined horizon. It rose with amazing rapidity, a mighty ball of cold fire that bathed the entire countryside in its orange glow.

It was a time to behold with wonder in silence, words would have spoiled the magic.

Suddenly, Kent sensed his companion stiffen, her fingers tightening over his own.

'What. . .'

'Sshh! I heard something over there,' she whispered, pointed with her free hand to where the orchard boundary joined the edge of the wood.

He listened intently, heard a dry twig snap, a branch spring back as though somebody pushed their way through the trees. Rhododendron leaves rustled. It might be fox or badger, Kent thought, watching closely.

A figure emerged from the shadows into a patch of moonlight, lean and furtive. The stranger wore trunk hose and canions that were not befitting either vagrant or poacher, carried a pole from which a hook dangled. A river poacher, perhaps, on his way to lift an illicit trout from some manorial stream. In which case it was no business of Guy Kent's even though the other dressed above his status in life.

'It's. . .' Diana stared into the half light, 'it's *Robert the Angler!*'

It was Kent's turn to *sssh*. He held up a hand for her to be silent, whispered in her ear, 'Watch and see what he does.'

'He's going to steal your canions, that's what,' she hissed back. 'And good luck to him. I doubt whether even Robert will wish to walk around with bloodstains on his clothing!'

Robert moved into the orchard, darting runs between shadows, stopping to look around him. He was clearly nervous, a man of the nocturnal hours who eked a sparse existence by hooking clothing from washing lines with his fishing line and selling the cloth to passing tailors.

Guy Kent tensed like a coiled spring. The fellow was less than twenty yards from them, hidden by the twisted trunk of the old apple tree against which they had been sitting.

'Guy, no! It isn't worth—'

Kent's powerful leg muscles springboarded him into action, hurled him forward. But Robert lived by his alertness; the rustle of dry grasses had warned him that he was being observed, and in one movement he turned and ran. When his fishing rod caught on an obstructing branch he abandoned it, for it was but a matter of a few minutes' work to make another.

His long legs covered the ground with remarkable speed, twisting and weaving between the trees; he was accustomed to flight and had only once been apprehended. On the occasion when Bill Symes had lain in wait and grabbed him, Robert had had no illicit clothing in his sack, only his fishing rod; his claim that he had been on his way to fish in the common stream had earned him a reprimand. The penalty for thieving was the gallows. He was determined never to be caught again.

Kent knew that his quarry would head back to the wood whence he had come, and once amidst the trees would surely escape, maybe climb up on to a low bough and lie still. Or merely crouch in the undergrowth whilst his pursuer passed him by.

Kent opted for a diagonal course to the left of the other, for he was closer to the wood than Robert. The latter glanced round, wavered in his flight and, realising that his escape route had been cut off, turned back for the orchard.

A chase through the old fruit trees; right and then left, forward and backward, hounds quartering a stag, sticking to its trail until finally it collapsed in a state of exhaustion.

Robert was clearly tiring, he seldom ran more than a hundred yards before his pursuers gave up the chase. He was breathing hard, frightened. This had never happened to him before.

Once, when an avenue of escape beckoned and he seemed to have outdistanced the one on his heels, Diana appeared from behind a tree, drove him back in the opposite direction. His resolve was fading along with his stamina. He remembered how he had bluffed Constable Symes and halted, waited.

'Well, well!' Kent did not even appear to be breathless; he looked almost debonair standing there in a shaft of moonlight. 'If it isn't Robert the Angler, caught in the act of stealing my canions from the washing line!'

'No, no, sir.' Robert's denial came out in a gasp. 'Indeed, I was not about to steal your canions. I was on my way to try for a fish in. . . in the common stream and—'

'The common stream is a good mile *that* way.' Kent pointed beyond the shadowy wood. 'Perhaps, then, you lost your way?'

'Yes, yes, I was lost, that is correct.'

'You're not only a thief, but a liar, too!' Kent's attitude became stern. He heard Diana coming up behind him. 'Miss Hawker will testify that we both saw you attempting to steal from our washing line. I suggest that you give me no more trouble and accompany me to the town hall where, doubtless, Constable Symes or one of his deputies will be on duty.'

'No, sir, *please*. I dare not be seen around the town. My very life would surely be forfeit!' A whine, a desperate plea that transcended a theft charge.

'You fear the gallows?'

'Yes. . . or a knife or a ball, perhaps whilst I am in the stocks. Please, sir, do not take me back to town. I will do anything you ask, tend your garden or cut logs, but. . . *please. hide me!'*

'I see.' Kent licked his lips, wished that there was a jar of camomile brew handy. 'You fear somebody might kill you, possibly in the stocks, just as they killed old Ned, eh?'

'Surely. Too many have died recently, and not because of the plague. Ned, Edmund the Monk, Jane, Nicholas, I hear, and even the highwayman. So why should they spare me?'

'I know not why they should either kill you or spare you. You had better tell me, Robert.'

'I dare not, sir.'

'Then Constable Symes it is!' Kent grabbed the other roughly by the arm. 'If you refuse to tell me, then you can tell *him!'*

'*No!*' A half-scream. Robert tried to wrench himself free but it was futile against one of such deceptive strength. 'I will tell you, if you promise not to take me to the constable.'

'Very well, but only if you fulfil your promise.' Guy Kent relinquished his hold, tensed himself in case the other made a run for it. But it was only too clear that flight was the furthest thing from his captive's mind.

'They killed Ned the Beggar on account of what he saw that night. . . and *whom* he saw.' Robert glanced around as though he feared that there might be a hidden eavesdropper.

'And *whom* did he see, Robert?' Kent thrust his face close to the other for Robert the Angler's voice had dropped to a hoarse whisper.

'I do not know, sir, and pray God I never will else I am as dead as those corpses piling up in the charnel house.'

'Tell me from the beginning.' Kent folded his arms, leaned against a tree. Diana had moved up against him. Suddenly, a magical moonlit night had become one of stark terror.

'I was out and about that night, sir.' Robert shuffled his feet, looked

127

down at them. 'Going fishing.'

'No lies, please, Robert.'

'Well, I was passing by the charnel house which, as you know, adjoins Holy Trinity, when suddenly old Ned comes out of the dark screaming like I've never heard him before. Surely one o' the dead had risen up and was after him. My first thought was to hide. There were lights showing in the church and the door was open otherwise I might've run in there and sought the Lord's protection. But, no, something peculiar was happening in there. I knew I had to hide quick, then I saw the charnel wagon standing outside the church doorway and, quick as I could, I jumped on it and pulled some of them sacks that they use to cover the bodies over me. Yes, sir, I hid on the death cart and I was shaking so that it fair rattled.'

'Go on, Robert.'

'There was a chase, at least I think there was, somebody running after Ned but they never caught him. I know now that he went to the gypsies, and when they turned him away. Jane took him in. They killed her in case he had managed to tell her something in that signing way of his. They killed Ned in the stocks, just to make sure.'

'And you?'

'Me, I stopped right where I was, my legs were so weak. I couldn't've run ten yards. There I was, hiding under the sacks up the corner of the wagon, trembling so that it's a wonder they didn't hear me. But they were too busy to even think of looking under the sacks. Whoever chased Ned came back and went into the church. Then he came out again, started loading up the wagon, bags of things that clinked and rattled. *I know now that it was the church silver and gold!*'

'So that's how they got it away!' Kent pursed his lips in the darkness, whistled softly. 'The moonmen were executed for that theft. You think the man loading the wagon could have been Edmund the homeless monk?'

'I never saw him, sir. It could have been Edmund or it could have been any one of the townspeople. Me, I hid under those sacks and never once poked my head out, and can you blame me?'

'No, but why didn't you make a run for it when whoever was loading up the wagon went back inside the church for more?'

'As I've told you, my legs would not have got me far. And the fellow had got everything piled up in the porch, he didn't have to go out of sight of the wagon, he'd see me for sure.

'Of course. And when did you get off the wagon?'

'Not until we got to where we were going.'

'And where was that?' Kent resisted the urge to grab Robert and shake him. Edward Las had died within seconds of revealing the criminal's name.

'I've no idea, sir. It was a long journey. I don't know how I stopped from crying out with cramp, and I was shaken about until I vomited. But I didn't have any other choice but to stay right where I was because that man would surely have killed me if he'd found me. He drove like old Nick himself was after him, and day was just starting to break when he finally pulled up and got down.'

'And you remained hidden?'

'Until the wagon was empty, sir. Apart from the sacks under which I was hiding, and the Lord be praised he didn't look under them!' Robert was clearly terrified just in the telling of his story.

'And after the man had gone indoors, you climbed down. What then?'

'I jumped down and ran and hid in the bushes, sir. I'd no idea where I was, which way to go, so I let it get properly light before I sneaked away else I'd surely have become lost in a part of the country with which I was not familiar.'

'But you eventually returned to Stratford.'

'It took me two full days, and if I hadn't recognised the Welcombe Hills in the distance I might've gone on to. . . anywhere.'

'And you've no idea of the locality to which you travelled as a stowaway on the wagon, Robert?'

'None at all, although methinks it was north of Stratford. On the other hand, it could have been south.'

Kent struggled to contain his exasperation. 'All right, you were taken somewhere, you don't know where, but somehow, by good luck, you found your way back. But what sort of place was it to which this unknown stranger drove the charnel wagon?'

'A house, sir.'

'Yes, yes, but what sort of house?'

'A big one, sir. Maybe not quite as big as Lord Armdale's but not far off. Well, maybe half as big.'

'Were there any distinguishing features about the building?'

'Like what, sir?'

'Well.' Kent sighed; again he was so near and yet so far. 'Perhaps a coat of arms over the doorway?'

'There was one of them, sir, but I didn't take much notice of what it was like.'

Kent sighed again. Diana sensed his frustration.

'Oh, and there was a bird on the roof, sir, I couldn't help but notice it.'

'By now it will probably be safely at roost, Robert. I don't think that is going to help me much.'

'Not this one, sir. It roosts up there, all day and every night, never goes anywhere.'

'You talk in riddles, Robert. How can a bird, whatever its species, stay permanently on a roof? It would die of starvation within a few days.'

'Not this one, sir.'

'And why not?' Kent glanced up at the moon. Perhaps it had some nullifying effect on the other's brain.

'Because it's made of stone, sir. Huge, ten times the size of any other bird you've ever seen. Like a kind of hawk.'

Kent's expression was one of mingled amazement and incredulity. Even Robert the Angler backed away from it.

'Like a *hawk*, you say, Robert?'

'Yes, sir, a *giant* hawk.'

'All is suddenly crystal clear!' Guy Kent whirled, held Diana to him. 'There is only one giant hawk I know of that sits atop the roof of a country mansion. A stone falcon that was put there a century ago when the estate belonged to Lord Witherington who was a famous falconer in his day, lived for his sport. The house can be none other than Falcon Towers and its present owner obviously has every reason to plunder the church artefacts for I have heard whispers that his farming empire is failing, mostly due to the pattern left by feudalism, manorial organisation and the common field system of farming. Gentlemen were urged to go to the towns to seek their wealth, but it did not work. They were then persuaded to return to the country, only to find that their farms were run down and on the brink of bankruptcy. A man who lived well in London might return to his old home to find his fortune almost depleted. As doubtless did the owner of Falcon Towers!'

Both Robert the Angler and Diana stared at Guy Kent in amazement, not understanding. But he had no time to explain.

'Let Robert hide in the cottage until I return,' Kent turned away. 'We shall need his evidence, doubtless, for all the other witnesses and suspected witnesses have been murdered. Then, Diana, ride to the town hall and inform the constables where I have gone. Ask them to follow forthwith for I may well have need of a deputation of armed men! I dare not delay. Already I might be too late and the birds, with the exception of the stone falcon, have flown.'

Within minutes Guy Kent was mounted and armed, and heading south.

CHAPTER EIGHTEEN

Falcon Towers had once been a fine manorial house surrounded by rich farmland, the home of a hunting companion of Henry VIII. Now it was but a crumbling wreck of its former grandeur, scarcely recognisable to those who were once familiar with it except for the mighty bird of prey upon the lofty turreted roof. Sculpted by the finest craftsmen in the land, and rumoured to be a gift from the king in return for the sport which he had enjoyed here with his falcons, the statue still retained its pride. It surveyed its domain from above, gigantic and so lifelike that even the woodpigeons gave it a wide berth as they flew to and from the surrounding woodlands. The crows mobbed it but kept a wary distance in case those wings should open and the cruel talons rake the feathers from their flesh. It commanded the awe and respect of any who looked upon it, man or beast.

By daylight Falcon Towers was forbidding; by moonlight it was menacing, threatening all who looked upon it with its glowering windows and its cavernous portals, a stone effigy of some unholy monster that had once roamed the countryside. The stonework was worn smooth by the lashing gales of countless winters, weeds sprouted unchecked right up to the moss-covered sandstone terrace. It was a place of dereliction.

A place of the dead. Begone all who trespass here, enter at your peril!

Kent had left his horse down where the overgrown driveway joined the travellers' route to Oxford and London. An owl had hooted its derision at his arrival, for who but a fool or a madman would come here in the dead of night? Or a rogue.

The stallion cropped the dry grass unconcernedly as Kent stood listening. Everywhere was so still, footfalls would be magnified. He must move with extreme caution.

Rhododendron boughs overhung the winding driveway. He noted that several had been snapped or bent, hung down with the sap still oozing from them; a carriage had passed this way recently, and he knew by the angle at which the leafy boughs were bent that it had travelled in the direction of the big house. It had not returned. Yet.

He wondered how long it would take the constables to arrive. An hour, perhaps two, they were not renowned for their swiftness. Symes was a slothful fellow, who would not desert his bed readily; certainly he would not be inclined to hurry on Kent's behalf.

In the meantime there was much work to be done.

Kent's keen eyes scrutinised his surroundings, alert for a trap or ambush of any kind. The violent deaths of the coney-catcher and the parish clerk were fresh in his mind; his body still ached from his fall. He was determined not to be taken unawares next time.

His eyes took in the building and its dilapidation. The falcon seemed to exude evil; it was as though its stone eyes had picked him out and it was preparing to swoop down on its human prey. Something in the shadows attracted his attention. He peered. It was a caravan, pulled up close to the side entrance to Falcon Towers. A piebald in the traces munched the moonlit grass as if it needed to refresh itself after a lengthy journey, or perhaps it sensed that another was imminent. Either its owner had been too lazy or too tired to unhitch the animal or else it had been left in readiness for a swift departure from here.

A gypsy caravan parked at this remote mansion was a matter of no small puzzlement to the man who crouched beneath the overhanging boughs of the untended rhododendrons, but recognition of that red and yellow painted horse-drawn conveyance had him sliding his pistol out of his belt, his thumb resting on the hammer in readiness. The mystery deepened still further *for that was none other than Cornelius, the Romany leader's, caravan!*

Cornelius had supposedly departed the Welcombe Hills in the wake of his band. He had done so, but this was the last place in which Kent had expected to find him. Perhaps the owner of Falcon Towers secretly sympathised with the gypsies, had offered them sanctuary where they would not be harassed by the constables or the Witchfinder. No, he was not given to compassion – most certainly not after Kent's recent discoveries. Cornelius was here for a specific purpose, one that had Kent's nerves tautening, and he was grateful that he had come armed.

He debated whether or not to await the arrival of Constable Symes and his men, for surely they must by now have left Stratford. A sudden shaft of light beamed from a ground floor window. Whatever evil was planned for this night, it had already begun. If he held back now, the villains might well escape. Their cunning and treachery so far was unrivalled in his encounters with criminals; they had thwarted him at every turn, left a trail of corpses in their wake that was only surpassed by the plague itself. Kent could not risk waiting any longer.

Taking advantage of every patch of shadow, he crept forward, thanked the moss and weeds that covered the drive for muffling his footfalls.

He edged close to the caravan. The horse did not so much as raise its head. The wooden steps creaked beneath his weight and he paused again, but the only sound in the stillness of the night was the steady mastication of grass.

The door was ajar. He pushed it open, held his pistol at the ready. A moonbeam slanted in through the opening, allowed him to see the interior as clearly as if a candle had been lit.

Everywhere was neat and orderly, a compact household on wheels, not an inch of space wasted. He stiffened. The bed at the far end was surely occupied, a heap of hand-woven rugs wrapped around a slumbering human form.

He pushed the door still wider, allowed the moonlight to infiltrate fully until outlines became detailed. It was Raol who lay upon the bed, still wearing her multicoloured headscarf, her shawl wrapped around her as though her old bones felt the cold even at the height of summer. Her hands were folded across her bosom, her toothless mouth pouted but it did not dribble. Her eyes were closed.

Kent detected that only too familiar odour in the stuffy, confined space, and he knew why her bosom did not rise and fall with the rhythmic breathing of one who slept heavily.

He went back outside, the balmy night air nectar in his lungs. He eased himself along the stone wall until he came upon that lighted window. Cautiously, furtively, he peered inside.

Sheets covered the furniture as though it had not been used in aeons. Even the clock upon the marble mantelshelf was draped. There was nobody in sight although, even from here, he was able to discern footmarks in the thick dust on the floor where somebody had trodden to and from the door. The centre of the room was taken up with wooden crates and bulging sacks, stacked in the manner an

133

occupier might have used on the eve of vacating his dwelling. A lantern burned steadily on the table and Kent thought that he heard a murmur of voices from somewhere within.

The proverbial bird had not yet flown but it was stretching its wings in preparation.

As far as he knew, from hearsay which was not to be relied upon, the owner of Falcon Towers was a widower, his wife having passed away the winter before last. Pneumonia had claimed her, so it was said. The presence of servants was unlikely under the cloud of impending bankruptcy; the dereliction, the covered furniture, bespoke a neglect of household chores.

Kent considered the odds against him, located the servants' entrance around the first corner and was not surprised to find the door unlatched, for those whose villainy was nearing fruition would certainly not be expecting visitors in the dead of night. He held the advantage of surprise; the pending arrival of the constabulary was a bonus.

A long stone corridor stretched ahead of him. Moss grew upon the damp walls, and there was a suffocating smell of staleness as if the house had been unoccupied for several months. Which, in the light of recent revelations, Kent knew that it had.

The room in which the lantern burned upon the table undoubtedly lay beyond the first door on his left. He was already moving towards it when he became aware of heavy footfalls approaching from the opposite direction. A light showed round a bend in the passageway.

Kent darted back into the shadows, squeezed up against a stone pillar. A trail that had begun with degradation and murder in the town stocks had led him to a mansion of former affluence. Ned's death would not be in vain, he vowed, and cocked his pistol in readiness.

A lantern held aloft revealed two figures. The foremost was clearly Cornelius the Romany, the second was partly hidden behind his companion.

'You have done well, Cornelius. You will be handsomely rewarded for your help when you reach London. You are absolutely clear concerning your instructions?'

'Aye.' The gypsy's tones were guttural, there was an unwillingness about him as though he would do what he was bidden because he had no choice. 'I shall drive to Bishopsgate, which will take some considerable time, for loaded as I shall be I cannot risk the horse dying on me. There I shall be contacted by a man called Barnaby who will instruct me further.'

'And pay you a thousand groats for your trouble. And your silence. And your woman?'

'She will burn with the caravan when all is finished.'

'You are sure she did not die from typhus?' The other stepped back a pace, clearly concerned for his own safety. His features were bathed in shadow.

'Heart failure. Whenever she contacts the dead, it exhausts her. She appeared to revive after the last occasion and then, this evening, she just died. Her time was nigh. She has been a good woman; I cannot complain.'

'None will question a Romany on his travels. But on no account leave the caravan untended.'

'The dead will protect it.'

'Let us pray that the good Raol does just that, Cornelius, for should you be found to be carrying the church artefacts, none can save you from the gallows. Not even I.'

Cornelius's expression changed. He was holding the lantern at arm's length, peering into the darkness ahead of him. 'There is somebody here or else my senses fail me.'

'There is nobody here. Nobody would have any reason to suspect. The moonmen have been hanged for the crime, the monk was the perpetrator. Everybody who saw or guessed has been silenced.' The man standing in the shadow of his companion gave a forced laugh.

'I *smell* them,' the Romany's hairy nostrils flared, 'they are close, within this very house.'

Kent heard the metallic snap of a pistol being cocked. A moment of silence in which eyes were strained in his direction and he heard the stentorian breathing of the gypsy. The fellow was no rogue; he had been forced into this, or else bribed with a promise to exempt his people from persecution within the county boundaries. Whichever, he was still an accessary to robbery and murder and that made him a dangerous adversary.

'Go on ahead, Cornelius, and make sure there is nobody here!'

Cornelius shambled forward with the lantern, and pitch blackness engulfed his companion. Kent tensed. It was not the gypsy he wanted but the man who had spun the web that had enmeshed innocent people, who had taken their lives for his own greed, who wielded power behind a façade.

That was when Kent stepped from behind his pillar, his snaphance levelled. 'Stay, Cornelius, for I have no wish to put a ball through you. Stand aside. Do not try to hinder me, for I have the authority to arrest the one who forces you to transport the stolen church artefacts to London.'

A thunderous report vibrated the narrow passage, and a vivid tongue of flame briefly lit up all but the man who fired in a moment of panic. A split second seemed a full minute in which Kent saw the gypsy jerk and stagger, his swarthy features contorted with pain. Crumpling slowly, the lantern slipping from his grasp, crashing to the floor.

A darting shape beyond. Kent fired as Cornelius fell, knew only too well that he had missed his mark as his hastily aimed ball chipped splinters of stone from where the passageway bent to the right. Cursing aloud, yet pausing to recharge his weapon by the light from the spilled and burning oil. There was nothing here to ignite: the stone was damp, the flames would die down shortly. He did not even attempt to stamp them out, rammed powder and wadding down the pistol barrel, followed them with a ball.

Cornelius's upturned face stared at him, sightless eyes that seemed to plead forgiveness for the disgrace which he had brought upon his own kind. The persecution of the Romanies would be continued due to his weakness and folly.

Kent felt his way along the wall, an arm extended in case he met with an obstruction. He stumbled against a step, mounted the flight that led beyond. Then his feet trod a carpeted wooden floor, and the moonlight streaming in through a window showed him that he was in what had once been a banqueting room. Only the oval table remained; everything else was gone, doubtless sold to pay off mounting debts. Until there was nothing left and only the church treasures and the parochial funds remained.

A door at the far end stood open; beyond it he saw another flight of stairs. Footmarks in the dust revealed that the one he pursued had gone that way, perhaps seeking to throw off his hunter in a maze of passages and rooms.

The deserted house picked up the slightest echo. Kent knew that the other had already gained the second storey and was climbing still, as if seeking safety in height. A panic flight that must end when he ran out of floors.

There was always the possibility of an ambush, for this man knew every inch of the large household. Darkness was Kent's most valuable ally, for in those places where he could not see, neither could he be seen. He scanned every filter of moonlight, relied upon

136

his ears and those extraordinary senses that had saved his life on past occasions.

The trail led upwards to an attic. He took care in raising his head above the square aperture, pistol held in front of his face in anticipation of a rapid return shot should he survive the fire of his adversary.

The attic was brightly moonlit through gaping windows and a partial roof collapse. There was not enough shadow to hide a crouching man. Rafters had fallen in, providing a precarious stairway that led up to the open velvet sky above.

And Guy Kent knew without any doubt that it was to the turrets that Martyn Wylde had fled, determined to defend his heritage to the very last.

CHAPTER NINETEEN

Kent heard a slate slide. A moment or two of silence, and then it shattered on the ground far below. Another followed soon afterwards. The roof of Falcon Towers was in a very dangerous state of disrepair.

He looked at the broken rafters that leaned from the jagged hole above where he stood. Even a climb up there was perilous. Somehow the timbers had supported the churchwarden's weight, but they had probably been strained to their limit.

Outside that owl was hooting. Kent had lost all conception of time. He wondered how near or far the constables were. *If* they were coming at all. Symes was under no obligation to obey the orders of a herbalist who was not even recognised as a physician; if he had drunk heavily that night he may well have ordered her to go away. He could not possibly guess the extent of Martin Wylde's villainy; he risked the wrath of his employer on the word of one who flaunted the authority of the Lord Lieutenant. It could have been a hoax by Kent to salvage his pride.

Kent tested the flimsiness of the collapsed woodwork. A cross-piece bowed but it held; the next one was slightly firmer. He was sweating heavily. If he reached the top he risked exposing himself to a pistol ball.

He made it, raised his head slowly. The expected ball ploughed into the roof a yard away. Fragments of slate flew in all directions, and a number came loose, avalanched downwards. He heard them smashing on the terrace beneath.

Now he saw Wylde. The churchwarden was lying full length on the sloping roof, relying upon the firmness of his grip to pull him upwards, a foot at a time. He was within a couple of yards of that awesome stone falcon.

Guy Kent could have picked him off easily, sent the churchwarden's body rolling downwards, listened to it crunch to a shapeless mass on the ground below. But he would not even have shot Edward Las that way.

'There's nowhere left to go, Wylde!' he called.

'Damn you, Kent!' The churchwarden secured a grip on one of the scaly legs, hauled himself up by it. The bird seem to move, probably a trick of the moonlight. He sat beneath it, dangled his legs over the edge of the plinth and busied himself reloading his pistol. 'I should have killed you a long time ago.'

'Not that your hireling, the highwayman, didn't try.' Kent laughed humourlessly. 'My fortune was better than his.'

'I'll make a bargain with you, Kent. There's a king's ransom stacked on the floor downstairs, gold and silver, money too. The caravan is hitched and ready, all we have to do is to load up. Half's yours, we can travel together. London is a big place. A man can lose his identity.'

'No deal. If I wanted I could take the lot and be gone before Symes gets here. After I'd picked you off like a sitting pigeon. I think the parochial ledgers will prove that it was you who was misappropriating the taxes and tithes, not King. He found you out so you had him killed.'

'You're too clever for your own good, Kent.'

'It's taken me a long time to come up with the right answer; you hid your tracks well. Throw down your pistol, then climb back down.'

'To an appointment with the gallows?' Wylde laughed harshly. 'Better to die up here defending my own heritage. They'll only take it from me over my dead body. The Crown stole it from me, helped by the Church, with their *Dialogue on Civil and Uncivil Life*. They urged gentlemen such as me to leave the country and settle in the towns. You can see for yourself what happens to one's home and lands in one's absence. By the time they realised their mistake, and urged us gentlemen to return to the country, the damage was done. I only took what was rightly mine, a recompense. I hear that Shakespeare is invited to dine at the Lord Lieutenant's table. *I* never had any such invitation. The last of my line, now the Crown will seize my lands. Where is the justice you purport to uphold, Kent?'

Kent was sure that the great bird moved its head as if to plunge its hooked beak into the flesh of the man who had betrayed everything for which it stood. It appeared to waver, then it steadied.

'At least I will not suffer the ignominy of the gallows.' The churchwarden cocked his pistol. Still only one man stood between himself and a fortune waiting to be loaded on to the means to convey it to the capital. Before day broke Martyn Wylde could have disappeared for ever. Nobody would glance twice at the passing gypsy in his colourful caravan. He raised his pistol, his hand shaking.

Kent ducked in anticipation of the shot. This time the ball was much closer, splintered one of the broken rafters. The report rolled and echoed across the surrounding countryside. The owl stopped calling.

Wylde hooked an arm around a talon, attempted to reload. He would continue to shoot until his powder and shot were gone, and if he had not killed the man who stood between himself and wealth and freedom. . . He never thought in terms of failure.

'It was all going to pay off the moneylenders, Kent. That way I could have started afresh, maybe rebuilt Falcon Towers, tilled the fields again. I don't want wealth, just what is rightfully mine. But if I can't have that, then I'll have the life I deserve in the city. Anonymously.'

'Misguided priorities, Wylde,' Kent wondered how many shots the other had left.

'By your book, not by mine.'

The falcon had definitely shifted position, tilted forward. Perhaps it bowed its head in the shame that had been brought upon it. The bottom of the plinth had sunk to the level of the tiles, a six foot high monster that weighed all of three tons. Martyn Wylde clung on with one hand, tried to hold the pistol steady with the other.

Kent ducked again, but this time the shot was several yards off target; the shower of slates went over the gable end. The echo seemed to linger, a vibration in the windless atmosphere.

No, by God, those were horses' hooves and heading this way!

Kent contemplated climbing down, going to greet the constables. It was too risky. There might be another exit from Falcon Towers of which he knew nothing. The spider might escape from his own web at the death.

Guy Kent raised himself up again, this time head and shoulders above the gaping hole. Below him, like a miniature lead army fashioned for the amusement of the gentry's children, mounted constables were pushing their way through the overgrown driveway. The figure in the rear was slender, and sat her mount with some trepidation. He knew without any doubt that it was Diana Hawker.

A sudden vibration caused him to grab for his flimsy support; it slid but held, the rafter he stood upon bowed and strained. Ahead of him it was as though the entire roof was collapsing. Slates were sliding in their dozens. The stone plinth was askew, the mighty bird twisted to one side, its posture that of sudden anger, as if it tried to shake off the mortal who clung to its legs and prevented it from flying.

A noble bird of prey that had waited three parts of a century for its freedom strained; it even seemed in the mystic light of the waning moon that a wing flapped briefly. Perhaps if it followed the steep slope to where the drop began it could glide, regain its powers of flight at long last.

Miraculously, it did not topple. Somehow the base slid, a mass of gathered tiles keeping it upright.

Martyn Wylde clung on with both hands. His pistol was gone. It might have been the effigy that screamed its triumph.

The falcon swivelled as though trying to keep its footing, its prey held securely in its talons, a pathetic creature that fought and struggled, an unwary vole plucked from the ground by its deadliest foe.

On the very brink it halted momentarily, reared back up to its full height. Kent almost believed that it was about to take wing, but at the last moment its weight yielded to the law of gravity.

Its final departure was ignominious, a lurch and a stumble, a headfirst dive, its victim clutched tightly in its talons.

Then it was gone.

Kent braced himself for when it hit the ground below. Falcon Towers shuddered under the impact, and a section of the roof followed in the wake of its fallen talisman. Down below the horsemen huddled, shied from the remains of the broken bird which was bleeding profusely.

CHAPTER TWENTY

'I should be grateful if you would give me the facts, in chronological order, of this dastardly affair.' Richard ap Cynon put his fingertips together, leaned back in his chair, his eyes closed so that he appeared to be on the point of dozing. 'I am confused, to say the least, by the happenings and the outcome. It has been a great shock to me to discover that Martyn Wylde, a trusted landlord and churchwarden, had embarked upon a criminal venture of such magnitude. Of course, I was aware that his lands, like those of many others throughout England, had gone into decline. The changes brought about by our most noble Queen will, I have every confidence, restore the agricultural scene to its former wealth. But I digress. Pray proceed.'

'It would appear that Martyn Wylde had fallen into the clutches of one Barnaby Royle, an unscrupulous moneylender and receiver of stolen goods in London.' Kent spoke slowly. In some instances supposition would have to link known facts; some aspects of the case would never really be proved. 'Wylde supported his ailing estate with dubious borrowing from this man until Royle demanded repayment. In desperation, wishing to solve his financial problems and preserve his heritage and reputation, Wylde planned a cunning and audacious robbery. Had he not been seen by the beggar who was sleeping in the doorway of the adjacent charnel house, he would surely have succeeded. Witchcraft and satanism was the foil.'

'Hence my suspicions about the murder of a beggar being auspicious.' Those dark eyes flickered open, closed again.

'Quite, my lord. Ned escaped on the night, fled to the gypsy encampment but was turned away by Cornelius who had agreed to transport the stolen goods to Barnaby Royle in London. The beggar was then sheltered by Jane, and then, following his arrest by Constable Symes, was duly committed to the stocks where he was murdered.'

'By Wylde?'

'Almost certainly, for apart from Cornelius there was none other

141

involved in the plot and the gypsies were keeping clear of town. It would have been an easy task for the churchwarden to knife the beggar during the fight that broke out amongst some louts. But Wylde feared that the beggar might have conveyed that which he had witnessed to Jane. So, after I had successfully rescued her from the clutches of the Witchfinder, Wylde hanged her in her cottage. Edmund, the homeless monk, conveniently for the murderer, visited the cottage shortly afterwards and became the scapegoat, along with the moonmen who were just common thieves.'

'A miscarriage of justice that saddens me.'

'Myself, too, sir. Wylde was doubtless convinced that any who might have seen his nefarious activities were beyond talking. But, in order to ensure the monk's conviction, Nicholas, the coney-catcher, was handsomely bribed to perjure himself. So when it was known that I wished to question Nicholas, he, too, forfeited his life in the most improbable way by falling head first into one of the gamekeeper's mantraps. Such a foolish method of murder, but Wylde needed to create the impression of an accident; a knife or a ball in the back would have created further suspicion on top of the beggar's death.'

'The highwayman killed the coney-catcher?'

'Yes, just as he ambushed and shot Matthew King, the parish clerk, and clumsily faked a suicide.'

'Because King had discovered that the churchwarden was stealing from the parochial funds?'

'Precisely. Wylde saw a way to throw the blame on to King and silence him at the same time. Had Las had the brains to discharge the pistol against his victim's head, thereby leaving powder burns around the wound, he might have fooled me also. What is more plausible for one exposed as a thief than to take his own life rather than suffer the shame and ignominy of execution? I presume that King was riding to Warwick to seek audience with yourself to explain his findings but Wylde had already assigned the murderer to ensure that the parish clerk never reached his destination.'

'You are most astute, Kent. And how did Las, a notorious robber of travellers on lonely roads, come to associate with one in the position of churchwarden?'

'That I do not know, sir. Possibly Las waylaid Wylde and the churchwarden saw a means whereby he could both escape being robbed and have a ruthless killer at his command. My return to Stratford was of no small concern to Wylde and he sought to dispose of me. Doubtless, had I not survived Edward Las's ambush, the constables would have ridden to where he had his hideout, and Las would have been killed in the ensuing exchange of pistol fire. Then the way would have been clear for Martyn Wylde to transport his booty to London, his debts would have been paid, and he would have been free, following the termination of his elected period as churchwarden, to continue life as a respected and wealthy landowner. Unfortunately, on the night Wylde robbed and desecrated the church, he had an unwitting stowaway on the charnel wagon which he used to transport the artefacts back to Falcon Towers. Robert the Angler feared for his life because he knew why the others had died. It was by pure chance I caught him attempting to steal from my own washing line. I have promised him a pardon, sir; I hope that I am not being presumptious.'

'I shall endorse it,' Richard ap Cynon's eyes flickered open. 'You have done tolerably well, Kent, I heeded my intuition when I decided to return you to Stratford even though it appeared that the matter had been brought to a conclusion.'

'Thank you, my lord.'

'There was once a noble knight who lived within this county.' The Lord Lieutenant's eyes smiled mischievously for, on occasions, hearsay reached his own ears and he had heard that his man had pride in a mythical bloodline. 'His lady was named Phyllis and, although they were not married, he loved her dearly. So much, in fact, that he hated having to leave her behind when he embarked upon adventures in far places. He jousted and defeated both of the infamous German dukes, Otto and Rainer, and it is well known how he slew the Dun Cow not far from here. Single-handed he routed fifteen villains in France and fought bravely in the Siege of Arrascoun. He slew a dragon, too, saved England from the Danish giant Colbrand and cut off the head of the giant Ameraunt with his sword. But each time he returned to his homeland, there was another challenge awaiting him and he had to leave fair Phyllis to answer it.'

'I am well acquainted with the legends, sir.' Kent's thoughts turned to Diana and how she would be eagerly awaiting his return.

'Another strange business has arisen in your absence, Kent,' Richard ap Cynon turned to gaze out of the window so that the other would be unable to read his expression, 'some distance from here, and you may be absent for some time. . .'

Guy N. Smith Fan Club

Sheringham
West Street
Knighton
Powys LD7 1EN
Organiser: Sandra Sharp

| Annual | (UK): £15.00 | (USA): $30.00 |
| Life | (UK): £35.00 | (USA): $65.00 |

- ◆ Free subscription to *Graveyard Rendezvous*
  (the Guy N. Smith fanzine), the magazine for fans
  and aspiring writers
- ◆ Automatic invitations to launch parties
- ◆ Club events
- ◆ 10% discount on Guy N. Smith books by mail order
- ◆ Signed books
- ◆ T-shirts
- ◆ USA & foreign editions